A HORS

CHRISTMAS

MW01244848

James H. Lilley

© James H. Lilley
All rights reserved.

No part of this book may be reproduced, stored in a retrieval system or transmitted in any form, or by any means without the prior written permission of the publishers, except by a reviewer who may quote brief passages in a review to be printed in a newspaper, blog, journal, magazine, or website.

First printing 2019

All characters and events in this book are fictional, and any resemblance to events and/or persons, living or dead, is coincidental.

Cover design and artwork by Bonnie Cullom

Dedication

Dedicated to my wife, Jody, for the many wonderful years you've shared with me. You've been there for the good times and the heartbreak and with so many words of encouragement and love. That has always made our relationship special.

I've often said I won the lottery when you married me on December 2, 1995. Yet, in reality I believe it was on February 6, 1988 when, in spite of me making a joke about a date, you showed up and walked into my life to stay. Although at the time it was the last thing I expected, I wouldn't trade away a minute of our life together.

Acknowledgements

As always, thanks to Dean Clark, my on-call emergency computer wizard for his magical way of righting my disasters.

Thank you to Bruce Curley, proofreader and editor for his expertise in helping keep my words on the correct path.

Thank you to Bonnie Cullom for her masterful artwork and cover design.

One

There was a recognizable whistling sound as the whip cut through the air, followed by a resounding crack. But, it was the very distinct cry of a horse in pain that caused the young man to jerk his head and look to his left. He watched the husky man in the dark blue shirt and jeans raise the whip to strike the horse again.

His hand had barely moved when his wrist was caught in what felt like the jaws of a steel trap. He spun his head and saw the angry glare burning in the dark blue eyes of the young man beside him. Try as he might, he couldn't break the grip and free himself.

"You don't beat a horse, Mister," the young man snarled, the fire in his eyes blazing hotter with each passing second.

"She's useless," the man snapped. "Can't be trained to do anything."

"You don't train a horse by beating it," he spat, moving even closer and tightening his grip. "Now, drop the whip."

By now the huge arena had fallen almost completely silent as onlookers wondered who dared to stand up to Bob Swanson. Known more as Bully Bob Swanson, he was notoriously ill tempered and a man few challenged verbally let alone physically.

Yet, today they witnessed a first when he somewhat meekly released his grip on the heavy leather whip and let it drop to the arena floor.

"I take it, since you brought this horse to the auction, you wanna get rid of her," the young man said, as he continued to hold Swanson by the wrist.

"Yeah. The only thing she'd be good for is dog food."

Although he didn't expect Bob Swanson to accept his offer he said, "Since you're so anxious to get rid of her, I'd like to make an opening bid of $20.00."

"Sold," he snapped, handing the lead line to the young man.

He stepped back three paces, reaching for his wallet, all the while keeping his eyes on Swanson. He pulled $20.00 from his wallet, but before handing the money to Swanson, turned to the man standing nearest to him.

"Sir, would you mind being witness to this transaction?"

"Uh... No. No, not at all."

With that he reached out and passed the bill to Swanson who jerked it from his hand and stuffed it in his left front pocket. "Okay, I just purchased this horse for the sum of twenty-dollars."

While Swanson stormed off in a huff, the man who witnessed the transaction extended his hand to the young man. "Son, it's sure a pleasure to meet you... Steve Whitfield."

For the first time the young man smiled. "Jackson Riley," he said as he shook Whitfield's hand.

"Mind if I ask what you're gonna do with your horse?

Now, Jackson laughed. "Well, I don't know. I don't have a place for either of us to stay and I don't think I can get her a room at the Hampton."

"You don't even have a horse trailer, do you?"

"Uh, no, sir. I was just passin' by when I saw the sign for the auction and just stopped in." He shrugged. "I've always loved horses and just planned on takin' a quick look at what was here."

"Were you headed any place special?"

"Well, Mr. Whitfield I was plannin' on tryin' to find a job

here in Cedar Falls."

Whitfield smiled. "I can help you. Got a nice barn where your horse can stay and a room and a job for you if you want it."

Jackson Riley stared at him for a few seconds. "Sir, I'd be a fool to turn you down."

"Good. Let's take your horse out and load her on my trailer and you can follow me back to the farm."

"Yes, Sir." He nodded. "And thank you."

When Jackson reached to pick up the jacket he'd dropped to the floor before he'd grabbed hold of Swanson, Whitfield saw the letters U. S.M.C. tattooed on his right bicep.

"Still in the Marines?"

"Not on active duty, but still a Marine."

Whitfield smiled. "Ah, once a Marine always a Marine."

"Yes, Sir," he replied, smiling.

"What're you gonna call your horse?"

He paused for a moment and looked at the Buckskin mare. "Well, sir, the Christmas season's almost here, so I think I'll call her Christmas."

Whitfield nodded. "You know, I like that. Yeah, I do, and very appropriate."

Whitfield studied the young man closely as they walked to the parking lot. He was close to six feet tall and probably weighed about 215 pounds. He talked softly to the horse until they reached the trailer. There he gently ran his hand up and down her face, from forelock to nose and kissed her before leading her into the trailer.

Whitfield nodded and smiled, thinking, *I like this young man. I hope I can keep him around for a while.*

It was almost a thirty-minute drive from the auction site to the Whitfield farm. The first thing that caught Jackson's eye was the twin stone pillars on each side of the driveway. Resting atop each pillar was a life-sized, chainsaw carving of a Quarter Horse, one black, the other golden brown with dark brown mane and tail. The black one on the left had his right hoof raised as if preparing to paw at the ground. The golden brown's head was turned slightly to the left, ears up as though he was aware of someone approaching.

He didn't have time to look over the entire property as they drove in, but he'd find time later. He did get a view of the barn as he drove up and it was obvious it was very well maintained.

Before he knew it, he had walked Christmas to a stall at the far end of the barn and Mr. Whitfield had already carried in three flakes of fresh hay. Next, a sizable portion of grain in one bucket and two five-gallon buckets of water were placed in the stall for her.

When he closed the gate to the stall, Christmas walked over, eased her head forward and lowered it to his shoulder. She stood there, head on his shoulder as her face just touched the left side of his face and head. She remained there for a short time before slowly backing away and returning to the grain bucket.

"Son, she's gonna attach herself to you like she was glued to you."

He smiled. "Well, Sir, I guess that means she won't cheat on me."

Whitfield laughed. "Come on. I'll take you to the house and help you get your bags in and then we can have lunch."

"You don't hafta go to all that trouble, Mr. Whitfield. You've already done more than enough for me."

"Nonsense. It's no trouble at all."

The house was a two-story log cabin with a porch that ran the length of the front and wrapped around and down the right and left sides. Jackson was led to the back of the house where he found he'd have a private entrance. His room, with full bath, held welcoming warmth that certainly fit Mr. Whitfield's personality. There was a double bed, with posts and headboard that matched the log décor. A recliner, TV, a desk against the back wall and a spacious walk-in closet completed his living quarters.

"Wow! This is really beautiful, " he said, looking around the room a second time.

"Why don't you drop your bags and I'll give you a quick tour of the downstairs and then we can have lunch."

"Yes, Sir."

Jackson wasn't expecting the sheer breathtaking beauty of the home, especially the area just inside the main entrance. The room itself was enormous and included what was obviously the living room and dining room. The cathedral ceiling stretched up for what seemed like forever and log beams ran from front side to back side, interlocking with the logs of the ceiling.

But, it was the stone fireplace that caused Jackson to stop and stare. It was centered perfectly against the outside wall, the stone rising upward to meet the logs at the top of the house. There was a light colored oak mantle reaching across the front that held about a dozen portraits of what he took to be family members and, of course, photos of a horse or two. There was a rotisserie for cooking over the fire and an ample supply of seasoned mesquite wood stacked neatly in a wrought iron bin.

A few minutes later he was seated at the kitchen table with Mr. Whitfield enjoying a chicken sandwich, potato salad and a glass of water.

Whitfield cleared the table, filled Jackson's water glass and said, "Are you new to this area?"

"Not really. I was born in River's Edge, but spent most of my time, fifth through 12th grades, growing up at a military school. That's where I found my love for horses."

"What about after high school?"

Jackson took a sip of water and went on. "I went to college for two years, but I started to get restless during the second semester of my sophomore year. I finished the semester and enlisted in the Marine Corps and served six years. I guess all those years in military school kept callin' me to go back to the military life."

"Why'd you leave the Corps?"

"I was seriously thinkin' about a career in the Corps when I saw a state police recruiting poster. I called and they sent me an application and then I took a few days leave to tackle the written test and their physical agility test."

Whitfield smiled. "I doubt that you had any trouble with the physical part."

"No, Sir."

"Did you get the job?

"Yes, Sir. But, the academy doesn't start until the first week of June."

"Well, if you want it and don't mind what's sometimes hard work tending the horses and keepin' up the barn, you have a job here until it's time to go."

"Never been afraid of hard labor, Mr. Whitfield."

"You won't hafta worry about cleanin' stalls, except on the weekends. I have two young men who come by every weekday for that chore."

Jackson pushed his chair back. "Why don't you give me a tour of the barn and grounds so I can get to know the farm?"

"You have warm clothes?

"Oh, yes, Sir."

"Good. Expecting another snowfall in a day or two."

Soon, Steve Whitfield was taking Jackson Riley on a guided tour of the grounds and buildings. They casually walked from the expansive indoor arena, to the hay and grain barn, storage barn and finally to the horse barn.

As they walked in Christmas stuck her head over the stall gate and Jackson stopped long enough to gently scratch her behind the ears and give her a kiss on the nose. She responded by licking him under the chin.

Mr. Whitfield shook his head and smiled. "I've never seen a horse take to anybody the way she's taken to you. I have a feelin' she's gonna do anything you want her to."

He nodded. "She's a good horse. Swanson just couldn't see it in her, and I have a feelin' this girl's a lot easier to train than he thought."

"Yeah, and I have a feeling you're gonna find that out and very soon."

They walked from stall to stall where Jackson was introduced to each horse. The gates to their respective stalls had a laminated paper attached with the name of the horse, its owner and their full contact information. In addition, it noted their daily diet and any required medications or supplements. Also affixed to each gate was a pocketed basic grooming kit that held various combs, brushes, hoof picks and treats.

At the end of the barn, across from Christmas's stall, there was a large bay lined with neatly labeled containers of grain, and an array of smaller containers for medications and supplements. There was a sturdy wooden divider that ran from floor to ceiling, which separated the tack room from the grain area. The room was filled with an assortment of Western and English Saddles, bridles, halters, bits, lead lines, tethering ropes and a huge trunk filled with different leather conditioners and cleaners.

A chorus of meows just outside the tack room caught their attention.

They stepped out of the room and Whitfield grinned. "Well, let me introduce you to the barn cats. The bigger black and white cat is Sylvester and the smaller one is Sylvia. Now, that big ole mean lookin', battle scarred Tom is Hank. He's kinda like the King of Whitfield Acres and he'll let you know pretty quick that he's the boss."

"Yeah, he looks like he'd probably take on a mountain lion and I have a feelin' he might come out the winner."

"Oh, count on it."

Jackson took a quick glance around and said, "I haven't seen any dogs."

Whitfield laughed. "They're here. They're just hiding from you. Now, I didn't train 'em to do this, but they like to hide from the new people and visitors. Then when they get the chance, they like to sneak up behind them and give a loud bark. Almost scared the pants off a few."

He looked around, gave a quick whistle and waited. A few seconds later there was a faint whisper of a rustling noise in the tack room and two muscular dogs strolled casually out and sat down in the aisle. Both were black with a sprinkling of tan and white on their chests and legs, but the breed was certainly a mixture.

Jackson grinned. "I don't' think they need to bark to scare the pants off somebody. They look intimidating."

"As soon as they get to know you, you won't need to worry. Give 'em a treat and they're as good as yours."

"I'll do my best to remember that" he said with a nod. "By the way, what're their names?"

"Rooster and Rita. They're brother and sister."

"Mr. Whitfield, if you don't mind I'd like to change into my barn clothes and boots, and get myself acquainted with the place. Then I'd like to spend some time grooming my horse."

"That's fine. I'll call you when it's dinner time."

Believing he was intruding he was about to object, but the look in Mr. Whitfield's eyes said otherwise. He walked back to the house changed clothes and returned to the barn.

He walked from stall to stall and spent a little time looking over the charts. In a matter of about 30 minutes he had memorized the names of the horses and their entire diets.

Soon he went to work, emptying, cleaning and refilling water buckets in each stall. Next he put hay in the stalls and filled dinner buckets with gain, being sure to add the proper supplements and medications as prescribed on their charts.

When he finished the chores, he gathered some grooming items from the tack room and took Christmas from her stall. He was about to put her in crossties when he decided to see if she'd follow his direction and not attempt to wander off.

He talked to her as he began softly brushing her forelock and face and it was immediately evident that she trusted the young man with the soothing voice. He combed out her mane and tail and began brushing her, beginning at her ears and working his way along her neck and down her body. He repeated the routine on her right side, all the while talking to her. He lost track of time, but completed his grooming just as Mr. Whitfield returned to the barn.

"Well, Jackson, ready to start getting the evening meal ready for everybody before we bring 'em in for the night?"

"Already took care of it, Mr. Whitfield."

"You put food out for everybody?"

"Yes, Sir. Hay and grain with supplements and medications just as listed on their charts and fresh water for all."

Whitfield shook his head and smiled. "Well, let's bring 'em in then."

Jackson turned, walked around Christmas toward her stall and said, "Come on, girl. Time for dinner."

Without a moment's hesitation she followed him into her stall and went to her grain bucket. He patted her on the side of the neck and she raised her head and looked at him for a few seconds before returning her attention to the grain.

"Okay, how long did it take to teach her that?"

"Walkin' to her stall?"

"Yes."

He grinned. "Well, whatever time it just took her to walk to the stall. I didn't tether her for grooming and she stayed there, so I thought I'd see if she'd follow me into the stall."

Whitfield slapped his hands together and started laughing rather loudly while shaking his head. "Ole Bully Bob Swanson was suckered by a horse. Yes, sir that beautiful mare took him for the ride of a lifetime just to get away from him."

"Sure glad I came along when I did. I hate to think of her bein' a can of dog food."

"Son, I'm beginning to think you comin' along when you did was sheer destiny, or the will of the Almighty."

Working side by side, it didn't take them long to round up ten horses and bring them in for the night. Then it was time to get cleaned up and ready for dinner.

Jackson walked into the kitchen where he was introduced to Rose Whitfield, Steve's wife. They definitely looked as though they were from completely opposite molds. She was quite beautiful and held a certain air of elegance. She was tall and slender, obviously physically fit, with perfectly styled hair and just the precise amount of makeup. Though he thought she would have been just as elegant and beautiful without it.

Steve, on the other hand, was at least three inches shorter and with his stocky build and down-home friendly manner, looked as if he'd be comfortably at home in a Country-Western bar. While he wore dusty cowboy boots, faded jeans and a flannel shirt to the dinner table, his wife wore black dress slacks, a red silk blouse and black high-heeled shoes.

Finally, he was introduced to Juanita, who was the cook, but from all appearances guessed that she was also a close friend. That thought proved to be true when she sat down at the dinner table with them.

After enjoying a delicious meal of tossed salad, Lasagna, oven baked bread and homemade apple pie, Rose helped Juanita in the kitchen, while her husband and Jackson sipped a cold beer in front of the fireplace.

Jackson and Mr. Whitfield talked for almost two hours, with the primary topic being horses and the work Jackson would be doing around the farm. They talked until the fire dwindled down to a few smoldering embers before they said goodnight.

Two

Within a matter of days, Jackson Riley was becoming well known around Cedar Falls. He visited the barbershop and instantly found a friend in Sid Watkins. Finding new friends seemed easy and he enjoyed talking with the waitresses at the town diner, the owners of Cedar Falls Fresh Bread and Pastries Shop, and the staff at Cedar Falls Tack Shop.

He also found that Rooster and Rita quickly became his new canine companions. Now, each morning in the barn with Rooster on his left and Rita on his right lying on their backs, he gave each a start the day tummy rub. Not to be outdone, the three cats began standing side by side, performing a dance ritual and meowing while waiting for their morning feeding.

In no time he knew each horse by name and spoke to them as he gave them their morning grain. When they completed their meal, Mr. Whitfield joined him in taking the horses out to their respective pastures.

As for Christmas, she found the love and attention she so much deserved and it was obvious she was attached to the man who rescued her. Jackson trained her to close her stall gate and when she went in, he'd wait until hearing the very familiar click of the lock before walking away.

Mr. Whitfield was amazed that she learned to close her stall gate in only a minute. He jokingly asked Jackson if he was going to teach her to drive his pickup truck.

With Mr. Whitfield's blessing, Jackson began cleaning up and repairing an old wagon in the storage barn. He especially liked the young man's idea of putting Christmas decorations on the wagon and, when the grandchildren were visiting, hooking up the two draft horses and taking them for a ride around the property.

Whitfield would often stop by in the evening when Jackson was working on the wagon and marvel at the young man's work ethic. He sometimes thought he looked as if he'd set his mind and body in a preprogramed mode and was more like a machine working than a man. Yet, he was quickly restoring the old wagon and it was beginning to show its once beautiful luster.

He also wondered if Jackson kept himself occupied in hopes of avoiding or chasing away the demons that had called a few times since his arrival. He'd heard him cry out and was certain the demon that taunted him was from his days as a Marine. Yet, he didn't dare ask, for fear that he might cause the young man to leave and surely, he didn't want that to happen.

Naturally, Jackson sometimes brought Christmas into the old storage barn while he worked. She would stand on one side or the other, content to watch him work and enjoy the occasional kiss on the nose or gentle scratching of her face he paused to give her. But, every now and then she'd move closer, rest her head on his shoulder as if trying to see the progress he'd made.

***

Taylor Whitfield arrived home on the first Sunday of Advent and was greeted by her parents, brother, Andrew, sister-in-law, Beth, nephew, Josh and niece, Anna. After having lunch with her family, she decided she wanted to go horseback riding.

She changed clothes and was out the door and headed to the barn before her father had the opportunity to tell her about Jackson.

She entered the barn and walked directly toward the far end when she heard the sounds in the tack room. Taylor paused briefly in the doorway, watching the man who looked as though he'd been hard at work rearranging the tack room. His face was covered in dust and beads of perspiration trickled over it leaving a path in the grime as it rolled down his face.

When he failed to acknowledge her presence she said, "Go saddle my horse."

He didn't respond immediately, but hoisted a saddle up and placed it on a shelf. He then turned and was surprised to see a very beautiful young woman with blonde hair, dressed in riding garb and holding a riding crop in her left hand.

Before he could say a word, she snapped, "Saddle my horse."

He stared at her and said, "Let me move some of this mess out of the way and…"

"No. I want my horse saddled now."

He took a deep breath. "Careful, young lady, you're gonna overheat if you don't calm down."

"Overheat?" she said, her voice rising a few octaves.

"Yes, ma'am. Keep this up and your gonna hit the boiling point."

"Oh, I'm already far beyond the boiling point," she snapped, glaring at him. "Now, go saddle my horse."

"Well, you need to cool off first."

An instant later he swept her up into his arms, turned and walked toward the barn door.

Momentarily stunned by his reaction, she froze. When she finally tried to free herself from him, he had already carried her outside. A quick turn to his left and he stopped and said, "This should help you cool down."

With that, and in spite of her struggling to free herself, he dropped her into a freshly filled water trough and stepped back, watching her flail her arms while she tried to grab the sides of the trough.

He moved closer and extended his hand. "Want a little help gettin' outta there?"

"Don't you dare touch me," she screamed.

"If that's what you want. But I don't think you can get outta there without a little help."

"I don't need your help," she yelled. "I... I don't want your help."

"If you change your mind, I'll be in the tack room."

He went back inside and began cleaning a Western Saddle while listening to her splashing and damning him. He smiled and continued rubbing saddle soap into the leather.

"Come out here and help me," she yelled to him.

He slowly walked out the door and looked at her. Her hair was a mess and it appeared that tiny ice crystals were forming on her headband. In a way she almost looked pitiful as she stared up at him, but he couldn't resist the urge.

"I bet that's cold."

"You know it's cold. Now get me outta here."

"Did I hear a please with that?"

She looked up and glared at him, wishing she could in some way retaliate, but whispered, "Please" instead.

As effortlessly as he'd picked her up and carried her to the trough, he scooped her out and carried her into the barn. He put her down on the tack room floor and wrapped two blankets around her. A moment later he had a towel and began wiping the water from her face and ice crystals from her hair.

"You'd better go and get outta those wet clothes and into a hot shower," he said, as he looked into her eyes... her very beautiful blue eyes.

Moments later she stomped through the front door of the

house and all eyes turned her way.

"My God, Taylor!" her mother blurted as she jumped to her feet. "What happened?

She dropped the blankets to the floor and half sobbed, half screamed, "He... He... That... that man at the barn threw me in a horse trough."

Her brother burst out laughing and her father was struggling to keep his composure, but couldn't hide the smile on his face. Her sister-in-law seemed bewildered and her nephew and niece glanced at her for only a few seconds and turned their attention back to the books they had been reading.

Her mother though was outraged. "Steven, you go down there right now, fire him and get him out of this house."

"Rose, let's discuss this in the kitchen," he said as he took her by the arm. "And, Taylor, you go get outta those wet clothes."

The instant the kitchen door closed, Rose said, "Steven, I want..."

"Stop right there. I won't fire him and I won't throw him out of the house."

"He... He threw our daughter in a water trough."

"Yes, and she probably deserved it."

"How... How can you say that?"

He took a deep breath. "Rose, let's face it, when Taylor saw him she probably decided to convince him she was the boss. That's the way she's always been, but this time she ran into somebody who didn't jump when she yelled jump."

"But..."

"When he didn't snap to attention, bow to her and beg to be her slave, she lost her temper like she always does and ended up in the water trough."

"Steven, I can't believe you're gonna let him get away with this."

"Oh, I'm not only gonna let him get away with it, I think I'll congratulate him for teaching her a lesson."

Frustrated, she threw her hands in the air. "This is just... just preposterous."

"Really? Rose, she's a carbon copy of you when you were her age. She's almost a complete duplicate of what you were when we first met. But you changed."

"You didn't throw me in a water trough."

"That's because one wasn't close by."

He turned and briskly walked from the kitchen and she knew the discussion was over. Whether she liked it or not, Jackson Riley was staying.

By the time she reached the living room, Steven was already on his way to the barn. A quick glance around the room told her everyone knew who had won the debate.

Jackson had just put the last saddle back in its place when Mr. Whitfield walked in. He looked at him and wondered what the odd smile was about.

"Well, I see you had the pleasure of meeting my daughter."

"Uh... Your daughter? You mean the young woman I threw in the water trough was your daughter?"

"Yes and..."

"Oh, Mr. Whitfield, I'm sorry. I didn't know..."

"Hey, no need to apologize."

"You mean you're not angry?"

"Not in the least, Jackson. I'm sure she deserved it."

"Well, I should apologize to her."

He shook his head. "On, no. Whatever you do, don't give in and apologize. If you say you're sorry she'll become the biggest pain in the backside you ever met."

He shrugged. "If that's what you want, Mr. Whitfield, I'll abide by your wishes.

Whitfield smiled. "Good. Let's get the horses in. Then we can go get cleaned up for dinner."

***

Prior to sitting down around the table in the dining room, Steve Whitfield introduced Jackson to everyone—everyone that is, except Taylor.

He took his daughter by the hand and said, "Taylor, I don't believe there's any need to introduce the two of you. I understand you met Jackson earlier today and your meeting was quite a splash."

She tried to pull away, but her father was having none of that. He politely pulled out her chair and she followed his urging and sat. When she looked up, she saw that he'd purposely seated her across from Jackson. She quickly lowered her head, but not before seeing the somewhat devilish smile on Jackson's face.

The meal itself proceeded without incident and soon they were enjoying another of Juanita's delicious home cooked dinners. Today she'd prepared roasted chicken, mashed potatoes, gravy, and mixed vegetables. But, for the children there were chicken tenders and French-Fried potatoes. Dessert today was fresh from the oven cherry pie with a side of vanilla ice cream. Josh and Anna passed on the pie and asked for ice cream only. Of course, Josh wanted a very generous serving of chocolate syrup over his.

During the meal it was evident that Jackson was very quickly gaining a fan club in Josh and Anna. They were enjoying the fact that he talked with them when they asked questions, but when he asked if they'd like to go horseback riding with him after dinner, the bond of attachment was sealed.

Over dessert, Andrew said, "Jackson, Dad, said you were in the Marine Corps. Thank you for your service."

"You're welcome. It was an honor to serve my country."

"Were you involved in any of the fighting?"

Jackson was quiet for a few seconds and all eyes turned to him. "Uh... I spent some time overseas."

Andrew realized he'd crossed into a very sensitive area and quickly changed the topic. "I also understand you've been accepted by the State Police."

He nodded. "But, I hafta wait 'til June for the academy to begin."

"I wish you luck."

After a little more casual chatter, Jackson said, "If you'll excuse me, I'll go change clothes and meet everybody at the barn."

Beth also left the table and took the children upstairs where they could put on something more suitable for horseback riding.

Andrew looked at his father and said, "I'm really sorry I said anything to Jackson about his time in the Marines."

"I know you weren't aware of what he'd been through." He looked around at each of them and went on. "Now, please keep what I'm about to say between us. I'm certain that young man has seen more horror than we would ever want to witness. I saw his Dress Blue Uniform in a clear garment bag and, from just a quick glimpse of his medals I know he was awarded a Silver Star, a Bronze Star and a Purple Heart."

Andrew shook his head. "Now, I can't even begin to imagine what it was like for him. I feel like a fool for asking."

"Andrew, I'm sure he knows you weren't tryin' to open old wounds."

"Yeah, but maybe I should explain..."

"I think it might be a topic best left alone."

"Okay, whatever you say," he said with a nod. "So, what else can you tell us about him?"

His father smiled. "Well, I can tell you Jackson sure has got a rock solid set of brass. He stood up to Ole Bully Bob Swanson and backed him down."

After a chorus of "wows" from around the table, including one from Taylor, he related the story of their first meeting and how Jackson ended up at the farm.

Taylor stared at her father. "He confronted Bob Swanson to defend a horse?"

"I've always said if you want to know a man's real character, watch him around children and animals. Children and animals are often better judges of a man's true nature than any man or woman could ever be." He pushed his chair back. "Now, why don't we go to the barn and watch the kids ride."

Rose said, "Steven, I have things to do here."

"Okay, dear."

When they arrived at the barn, Jackson had already saddled Christmas and the two ponies and was leading them to the indoor arena. It wasn't until everyone was inside the arena that they noticed the Santa Claus hat worn by Christmas.

The mood quickly seemed lighter and within a few moments Jackson, Josh and Anna were enjoying a leisurely ride. They talked as they circled the arena and there was little doubt that Jackson was very happy chatting with the children as they rode.

When the ride ended, they returned to the barn and continued their banter while allowing Christmas and the two ponies, Annabelle and Spiderman to cool down. After a good brushing, the ponies were returned to their stalls and given a peppermint treat.

Jackson gave Christmas a pat on the back and said, "Okay, girl, get in your house."

Everyone watched in awe as the Buckskin Mare turned and went into her stall. But, when she put her chin on the top rail of the gate and pulled until it closed, they shook their heads and began to cheer.

Yet, it was Taylor who blurted, "How did you train her to do that?"

He turned and said, "Well, I've always believed that when it comes to horses and dogs, love and kindness will accomplish a lot more than a beating. Then they learn and do things because they wanna please you, not because they're afraid of you." He paused a second, smiled and added. "I'm just happy her stall gate swings out to open. If it had been a slider like the rest, it probably would've taken a week to train her."

A moment later he walked to the stall, kissed Christmas on the nose and said, "Goodnight, sweetheart."

"Care to join us for a nightcap?"

"Thanks for the offer, Mr. Whitfield, but I wanna make sure things are ready for the morning feeding."

As they were leaving the barn, Taylor took her time ensuring she was last out the door. She paused, stood off in the shadows and watched Jackson walk from to stall to stall and say goodnight to each and every horse.

Later that night Taylor Whitfield stood in her darkened room and stared out at the snow-covered ground. She watched as strange shadows formed and disappeared when, from time to time, the moon peeked from behind the clouds.

Finally, she got into bed and stared up into the darkness and whispered, "Jackson Riley, I really wanna hate you. I really do, but right now you've got me confused."

Three

Jackson was up and out before sunrise heading into town and an early breakfast. After breakfast he stopped at Cedar Falls Fresh Breads and Pastries Shop and picked up coffee and an assortment of pastries to take back to the barn.

When he arrived at the barn, he found Jose and George there waiting patiently to begin cleaning stalls. He told them to relax and enjoy a coffee and pastry while he took the horses to pasture. They didn't argue and quickly helped themselves to hot coffee and a snack before beginning their chores.

Jackson returned and brought Christmas out of her stall for her morning grooming. He thought another coffee and maybe a cinnamon roll would provide a bit more energy for the tasks ahead. Between sips of coffee he brushed Christmas and, as always, talked to her as he groomed.

While he was busy grooming, Taylor walked into the barn, but stayed back and watched him. She was amazed at how gentle he was as he brushed her coat and the way he talked to her.

He paused and picked up the cinnamon roll, but before he

had the opportunity to taste it, Christmas leaned forward and took a healthy bite of it.

"Hey, that's my cinnamon roll you just took a bite of," he said, though it was obvious he wasn't angry.

Christmas looked at him and went on chewing the very tasty morsel she had stolen and it looked as if she was rather pleased with herself.

"Well, I hope you're happy. You certainly look quite proud of yourself."

Christmas just looked at him and he was certain she was actually smiling.

"Now, how would you like it if I went in there and helped myself to a handful or two of your grain?"

She shook her head up and down three times as if giving him approval to eat her grain.

"Keep it up and you'll turn into one of those junk food nuts," he said, while shaking a finger at her. "Next thing you know you'll turn out like Sergeant Reckless, a real Pogey Bait Queen."

After that admonishment she leaned forward again and very quickly took another bite of the roll.

"Hey! That wasn't an invitation for you to just help yourself to my snack."

Although she tried her best not to laugh, Taylor finally let go and began laughing.

Jackson turned and saw her walking toward him and said, "Wow! You can laugh... and smile. I should take a quick picture because I'm not sure when or if I'll see this moment again."

"Well, I couldn't help it. And, I should've filmed what I saw because it was so amazing to see how you and your horse interact. I mean..." She suddenly stopped and turned away.

"Okay, I guess it's back to normal. Whatever that is?"

"Saddle my horse," she shot back.

"It's looks like this game is gonna go on for awhile, so I'd better ask how you want me to address you? Miss Whitfield? Miss Taylor? Or would you prefer Your Majesty?"

She spun and walked quickly toward him, raising her hand to strike him.

"Careful now," he said. "There's a film of ice over the water trough this morning."

"You wouldn't dare throw me in there again."

"Try me."

She lowered her hand, but repeated her demand. "Saddle my horse."

"Do you want me to ride him for you too?"

"You… You're the most irritating man I've ever met," she yelled.

Jose and George, who had been listening intently to the battle of words peeked out of the stalls they were cleaning. When they saw Taylor's back was to them, they gave a quick thumbs-up to Jackson.

"Well, you're the most obnoxious woman I've ever met. Are you naturally this obnoxious, or do you practice?"

"Oh… oh… I hate you."

He smiled. "Look, I'll meet you halfway. You bring Bronson in and I'll help saddle him."

She brushed by him and returned a few minutes later with her horse beside her. She stopped just inside the barn door, but Bronson kept walking until he was close enough to nuzzle Christmas. Soon they were rubbing noses and it was evident there was a romance in bloom.

Bronson, too, was a Quarter Horse. He was a magnificent, well-muscled, black stallion with just a flash of white below his forelock.

Jackson ended the romantic interlude when he told Christmas to get in her house. She turned and went into her stall and, just as she had the night before, pulled the gate shut.

As promised, he worked with Taylor and helped her saddle

her horse. When Bronson was prepped for riding, Jackson offered to give Taylor a leg up.

"You're not gonna throw me over the other side, are you?"

He looked directly into her eyes and, once again, she caught just a hint of a devilish smile on his face.

"Don't tempt me, Your Majesty," he said while helping her mount her horse.

She glanced down at him. "You... You're... Oh, never mind."

"Enjoy your ride. And be careful."

When she exited the barn, Jose and George stopped their work long enough to give Jackson a round of applause. He bowed to acknowledge their salute and turned his attention to grooming Christmas.

***

Steve and Rose were seated at the kitchen table and pouring their second cup of coffee. After selecting a pastry from the tray Juanita placed on the table, Rose decided to bring up a topic from months ago.

"Steven, have you given any thought to your preference of the men Taylor has dated?

"Let's face it, it's difficult to offer an opinion about a man when she never dates the same guy twice."

"Oh, Steven, that's not true."

"Okay, when was the last time she dated someone a second time?"

"Well... There was... Uh..."

"See, you can't think of a time either."

"Certainly, those young men who have come by to take her out on a date..."

"Rose, Taylor doesn't date. She holds auditions, hoping to find that fantasy guy, 'Mr. Perfect', she's always talkin' about. Well, as far as I'm concerned 'Mr. Perfect' doesn't exist."

"She has high standards, that's all."

"Well, then she needs to compromise and bring her standards down to meet 'Mr. Reality'."

"I suppose your idea of 'Mr. Reality' is someone like this guy, Jackson Riley."

"From the impression I've gotten of the men who've come calling for Taylor, I doubt that if you combined them, they could survive a day in the world he came from."

"Well, I still wish you'd fire him."

"I won't fire him and that's not a topic open for debate. He's one of the hardest workers I've ever met. He's constantly busy in one way or another. When he's through feeding, he grooms his horse for two hours or more. After dinner he goes back and works on that old wagon. It's beginning to look like it's brand new. Now, he's asked if he can put up a heavy bag so he can work out when he's finished with everything else."

"Well, he might be doing all this extra just to try and impress you."

"No, Rose. I don't believe that's it at all. I think he does it to wear himself out so he can sleep. He works with a purpose and that's to push himself to the point of exhaustion. Then he hopes and prays that the devil won't come callin' and haunt his dreams after he falls asleep."

She was quiet for a few moments and then said, "I confess I have no idea what it would be like to live a day in the world he came from. And, I've heard him yelling in his sleep."

"I hope that by a stroke of luck, magic or a miracle, Taylor and Jackson raise a truce flag."

She shook her head. "After he threw her in the water trough it might take a miracle."

***

Jackson was returning to the barn after taking Christmas out to the pasture when Taylor walked in leading Bronson.

"Would you help me… please? Bronson cut his leg."

"How'd it happen?"

"He brushed against a broken tree branch."

He walked quickly to her and looked over the cut on the left rear hip. "Let's take him to the wash stall and get his saddle off and I'll see what I can do about that cut."

Once in the wash stall, Jackson was all business. He removed the saddle and placed it on the floor outside the stall. Next, he threw a blanket over Bronson to keep the chill off him. Then he carefully inspected the cut, which had stopped bleeding.

He soaked a cloth in warm water and began wiping away the blood, all the while talking to the horse. "Don't worry, big boy, I'm just gonna clean this off and then we'll see how bad this is. I don't think it's very deep and you probably won't need stitches."

After the blood had been wiped away, he had Taylor inspect the cut. She looked it over and nodded, agreeing with Jackson's assessment of the wound.

"You're right. I don't believe he needs stitches."

"We should cover the cut with some ointment, but I don't think it should be bandaged."

"I think you're right."

"It's up to you if you wanna call your vet and have him come look it over just to be safe."

She nodded. "I don't think that's really necessary."

"Okay. I'll help you brush him down and then I think you should let him stay in his stall, at least for today."

"Yes. Sure. I think that's a good idea."

Soon they were brushing the handsome stallion, he on the left while she brushed the right. They didn't talk, but as was his custom he talked to Bronson the entire time he brushed.

After the brushing he led Bronson to his stall, while Taylor walked beside him. Jackson led him into his stall and inspected the water buckets to make sure there was ample water. Next, he stood beside him and gently ran his hand up and down his face from nose to forelock.

"Now, Bronson, as your doctor, I'm prescribing bed rest and a carrot before dinner and an apple for dessert." He paused, smiled and said, "If that doesn't work, take two aspirin and call me in the morning."

Taylor quickly turned her head hoping he wouldn't see her smiling. A moment later she looked at Jackson and said, "What do I owe you for your help?"

Without hesitation he replied, "A smile would be nice."

She closed her eyes and shook her head. Suddenly she spun to her left and began briskly walking for the barn door. She paused long enough to call back to him, "Jackson Riley, you're impossible." Then she continued on her way.

"Impossible?" he muttered, looking back at Bronson. "How am I impossible?"

He retrieved a flake of hay and put it in Bronson's stall. As he closed the gate he said, "Man, I'm sure glad I didn't ask for a kiss. She would've probably beaten me with her riding crop."

Bronson shook his head up and down.

Jackson laughed. "Hey, you know her a lot better than I do."

Four

Over dinner Taylor told everyone how her car slid off the road after she'd hit a patch of black ice. She was uninjured, but the car suffered a significant amount of damage and, unfortunately, there were no rental cars or loaners available at the dealership. Frustrated, she had called her father and rode home with him without bothering to rent a car from the rental agencies in the immediate area.

Her luck didn't improve when her father said he had business appointments for the next few days and his car was unavailable. Her mother tossed the third strike when she informed Taylor she too had important errands for St. Martin's and St. Ann's Churches.

"You can use my pickup if you need to run errands," Jackson said.

She stared at him for a few seconds. "You'd trust me to drive your pickup truck?"

"I didn't say I'd trust you."

She began laughing and shook her head. "Would you please stop it?"

"Stop what?"

"Oh, nothing. Nothing." She reached for her water glass and saw the faint hint of a devilish smile on his face again.

After dinner, Jackson was off to the storage barn again to work on the old wagon. He spent about an hour and a half staining the right side before deciding to stop for the night and expend some energy on the heavy bag.

He walked Christmas to her stall and, once again, she closed the gate behind her. He rubbed her behind her ears, kissed her on the nose and said, "Goodnight my beautiful girl."

When he turned away from the stall, he saw Rooster and Rita lying on their backs and obviously hinting they wanted a tummy rub. He began giving them a tummy rub and soon the three cats appeared and watched the ritual soft scratching Jackson was giving the dogs.

After a minute he stood up and the cats started their dancing routine, meowing and tossing out their hint that a little extra food would be appreciated. He laughed and complied only to turn around and see the dogs looking up at him and wagging their tails. Now that surely meant they wanted a dog biscuit. He bowed to their wishes as well and returned to the storage barn.

There he took off his flannel shirt, put on the soft leather bag gloves and began striking the heavy bag. The routine was slow at first, but after a few minutes he began picking up the pace. Faster and more powerful blows struck the heavy canvas bag with a loud crack.

He moved right and then left, hands flashing out and back in the blink of an eye. Soon, his pace increased and he was attacking the bag with a savage fury, the blows landing with a heavy, dull thump that resonated throughout the barn.

He lost track of time as he continued his relentless attack on the bag. Suddenly he was aware of someone standing in the shadows near the entrance watching him. He slowed his pace, moved to his right using the bag as a shield and looked at the figure near the door.

Taylor stepped from the shadows and walked slowly toward him. As she drew nearer she saw the sweat pouring in rivers down his face and dripping on to the black, sleeveless tee shirt he wore. A few more steps and she saw the scar on his left shoulder. It covered his upper shoulder and disappeared under the shirt and she was now certain of why he'd been awarded a Purple Heart.

She then noticed the fire blazing in his eyes, a look she'd never before seen and a quick chill raced down her spine. This was a very different man than the one who'd unceremoniously thrown her in the horse trough and recently made her laugh.

He moved closer and said, "To what do I owe this honor?"

"I... I... Would you do me a favor?"

"Sure," he said as he pulled a small towel from his back pocket and wiped the sweat from his face.

"I promised a friend I'd stop by to see her and meet her first grade students at Cedar Falls Elementary School. I..."

"What time do you hafta be there?"

"Around 9:30."

"Take my truck."

"Uh... Would... Would you please drive me?"

He stared at her for a moment. "You want me to drive you?"

She lowered her head. "Yes. Please."

"Okay. I'll get an early start feeding in the morning and grab a quick shower afterward. Then we can go to breakfast. My treat."

"You don't hafta do that."

"Look, I promise I won't bite you. Even if I do, you don't hafta worry. I've had my rabies vaccination."

She couldn't hide her smile. "Oh... Okay."

"Well, I'll see you bright and early."

"Goodnight," she said as she turned and began to walk away. "Make sure you cool down and bundle up good when you go out, it's really cold."

"Thank you. I'll be sure and do that."

He dressed and went back into the barn, walking from stall to stall and biding all the horses goodnight. Of course, Christmas did get another kiss before he left.

True to his word, he'd fed the horses and turned them out to their pastures and was waiting in the hallway when Taylor walked down the stairs.

A few moments later he was opening the door to his Ford, F250, for Taylor, helping her step up into the passenger's seat.

"This is really a beautiful truck," she said. "And what color is this?"

"It's a Metallic Burgundy."

"How do you keep it so clean in this weather?"

He smiled. "During the winter I have it dry cleaned."

"Dry… Oh, you do not." She couldn't help but laugh. "God, you are just impossible."

"Okay, how am I impossible?"

"You… You're… Oh, never mind."

She looked out the window at the tall Pine trees, their limbs swaying in the breeze, causing the snow to fall from their branches. She closed her eyes, thinking, *What's happening? I thought I really hated him, but now I don't know. He's… He's… He's driving me crazy.*

When they entered the diner, Taylor was surprised to see the number of people who greeted him. He acknowledged each of them by name as they followed the waitress to a booth. When they were seated, she was certain the waitress winked at Jackson when she gave him a menu.

He turned to someone who was sitting at the counter. "Sid, I see you haven't put up the Christmas decorations yet."

"I'll have them up before the day's over. I promise. In fact, my wife's coming by to help."

"That's good. You don't want anybody labeling you as the Cedar Falls Grinch."

When breakfast was served, she looked across the table at his platter of Blueberry Pancakes, three eggs, bacon, rye toast and bowl of fruit and said, "Are you really gonna eat all of that?"

He shrugged. "Sure am. I worked up a very big appetite this morning. Well, usually every morning, afternoon and evening and sometimes in between meals."

"But, you're not fat. I mean, I don't think there's an ounce of fat on your entire body."

He couldn't resist temptation. "Now, how would you know that?"

She lowered her head and blushed. "Oh... You... You're a big..."

"Pain in the..."

"I wasn't gonna say that you were a pain in the... Oh, never mind."

After they'd eaten and finished a second cup of coffee, the waitress brought the check and placed it on the table in front of Jackson.

As he was reaching for it, Taylor grabbed it. "No, I'll treat."

"Now, wait a minute, I told you I'd treat."

She shook her head. "No, you're driving. I'll treat."

The waitress looked from Jackson to Taylor and said, "Well, are we having a lover's spat?"

Taylor blushed again and looked away. "And, the day's only beginning. What's next?"

"Maybe one of those first graders will ask you for a date?"

Suddenly she decided to play along. "Maybe I'll accept."

He laughed and soon they were on the way to Cedar Falls Elementary School. He surprised her when he made a quick stop, ran into a nearby store and rushed back out carrying a large box of candy canes.

"Who are those for?"

"The kids."

"Really?"

"Yes. Would you like one?"

"Uh... Maybe later."

They arrived at the school and, after notifying the school admin office of their presence, were escorted to Room 109. A moment later Taylor was introducing Jackson to her longtime friend, Diane Wilson.

Diane pulled her aside and whispered, "You finally landed a prize catch."

"What? Oh, no, Diane. No, it's nothing like that."

"Well, it should be."

Jackson became an instant hit when he handed out candy canes to the children and then offered one to Diane and Taylor. Both accepted and soon Taylor was telling the children about the Whitfield farm, the horses, dogs and cats. Of course, she was very quickly bombarded with questions about riding, feeding and caring for the horses.

Jackson slipped quietly into the hallway and made a call to Steve Whitfield. Following a brief conversation, he returned to the classroom.

When Taylor finished speaking, he whispered something to her and said, "Okay, kids, how would you like to visit the Whitfield Farm, see the horses and take a ride in a big wagon?"

The response to his question could almost be described as a vocal riot. The cheers and screams of delight echoed about the room and managed to bring the Principal and Vice-Principal running to the classroom only to find everything was under control.

Diane took Jackson by the arm. "Will I be able to ride in the wagon?"

"Sure. Older kids are allowed on board."

She squeezed his arm a little tighter. "If you're the driver, I'd like to sit next to you."

"Uh, we might be able to arrange that."

He glanced over at Taylor and the look on her face surprised him. *Whoa. Is she jealous?* He broke away from Diane, walked over and stood beside Taylor.

A moment later the urge was too overwhelming and he said, "You should've told them how much fun it is to swim in the horse trough."

She turned quickly and slapped him on the shoulder, but it seemed more of a playful slap than one of anger. Then, for just a fleeting instant, a hint of a smile showed on her face.

Prior to leaving, Jackson told Diane that Mr. Whitfield would provide transportation from the school to the farm Friday evening for those attending the "wagon ride." Naturally, the transportation would include parents who wanted to enjoy the outing as well.

Jackson and Taylor bade farewell to Diane and were soon on their way back to the farm. Jackson, however, said they needed to make a stop to pick up fresh carrots and apples for the horses.

Taylor accompanied him into the store and wondered why he was picking up more candy canes. "Need to feed your sweet tooth?"

"No. Just picking some up for Friday night to hand out to the kids again... and their parents if they'd like one."

Once back in the truck and headed home she said, "Why are you doing this for those kids? The candy canes? The wagon rides?"

He shrugged. "I thought it might add a little more fun to the Christmas season for them."

"Is this something you did when you were younger?

He was quiet for a few seconds then said, "No."

"What did you do when you were their age that made the Christmas season more fun?"

Suddenly, he seemed tense and she noticed that he gripped the steering wheel a little tighter.

When he didn't answer she asked again. "Come on, what made Christmas fun for you?"

Again, he was silent, but finally glanced over at her. "Uh, that's a... a... It's a bad topic."

Without thinking, she said, "Oh, I'm sorry. But if you feel like you wanna talk about it, I'd be willing to listen." Then she thought, *What am I doing? Why did I say that?*

"Let's just say it's something I don't like to talk about and leave it at that."

"Okay. If that's what you want."

But now she was intrigued and wondered what happened when he was younger. And, for whatever reason, she was very determined to find out.

Five

Later that morning Jackson brought Christmas into the barn for grooming. He was happy to see a new glow beginning to appear in her coat and he knew how much she loved the attention when she was being brushed and combed. Not to mention that almost endless "conversation" they shared, which of course meant she listened to him talk and occasionally gave a nod or a soft nicker of affection to show her approval.

Today when he began brushing her mane he said, "Well, girl, this morning Taylor opened the door to some bad times from long ago."

"I know she didn't do it intentionally, but it sure brought back a bundle of old hurt and heartaches. That wasn't a good time, even though Mom did her best to try and make things right. But, Dad just wouldn't stop drinkin' and he'd get really nasty and yell at Mom and me. He beat her too and sometimes he'd hit me. And his brothers and sisters blamed Mom for all the problems, but I know it wasn't her.

"Then just when I finished fourth grade, Dad went out of the house and drove off in the car. Mom tried to stop him, but he just pushed her aside and went out the door. A few hours later there was a knock at the door and a policeman came in and told Mom that Dad had been killed in a car accident. Lookin' back on that now it was a blessing that he hit a tree and killed himself and not some innocent family.

"Then things got really crazy. Dad's brothers and sisters told everybody that Mom was an unfit mother. Next thing I knew there was this court hearing and Dad's oldest brother and his wife were awarded custody of me because they lied and said Mom was the cause of all the family problems. The judge even ordered her to stay away from me and before I knew it, I couldn't even see her again. You know, sometimes I think some money was slipped under a table to bribe the judge."

He paused and took a drink of water and began to comb out her tail. "Anyway, it wasn't too long before Uncle Bill and Aunt Sue decided that havin' a kid around wasn't what they wanted. So, the next thing I knew I was off to military school. They came by a few times when I first started fifth grade, and then they just stopped comin' to see me. I spent the summers in a camp run by the military school and then back to the regular school grind in the fall.

"I didn't like it at first when I was sent away, but I got used to it after while. I know the discipline and the military training was good for me and I especially loved it when I started to learn about horses. I learned a lot about care and feeding and I really loved horseback riding. All through high school I had this very pretty mare I had to care for, but she wasn't as beautiful as you."

He paused once again, this time to give her a carrot and a kiss on the nose. "Nobody came to my graduation and before I knew it I was 18 years old and out on my own. I guess I was pretty smart by savin' almost all the money Uncle Bill sent me. I was able to find a cheap place to live and got a pretty decent job. I tried to find Mom, but she moved away and left no forwarding address, or at least that's what I was told.

"I tried college for two years, but it wasn't for me. I mean I was gettin' a good education and havin' a lotta fun with the girls in my classes. But I decided to enlist in the Marine Corps and before I knew it, I was standin' on those yellow footprints at Parris Island."

He heard a sharp yap, looked and saw Rooster and Rita lying in front of Christmas's stall, hinting that they were ready for another tummy rub.

He took a break from grooming Christmas and said, "You two are tryin' to push the limit on these tummy rubs." But he gave them a very hearty tummy rubbing anyway and then a biscuit, which he hoped would satisfy them for a while.

Next a chorus of meows said he had to open the treat drawer for Hank, Sylvester and Sylvia. "So, you guys had to get in on the act too." He tossed a catnip toy to each of them and figured they'd be stoned in no time.

He returned to brushing Christmas and began talking to her again. "I'm gonna go back and try and find Mom, but this time I'm gonna try her maiden name. Maybe keepin' her married name just caused too many ugly nightmares."

He lost track of time while he was grooming and talking with Christmas, but being with her was never a chore. He very lightly brushed her face with a soft bristled brush and continued to talk to her.

"I can't tell you how happy I am that I came along and found you. You didn't deserve to be mistreated or beaten with a whip." He laughed. "But it's sure a good thing that Mr. Whitfield was there and offered to take us in. If he hadn't you and me just might've ended up sleepin' behind a dumpster. Well, no matter what, I wouldn't have let you go."

He stopped for a second and listened to a song on the radio. "Now, that's a great song."

"You're a country music fan?" Taylor said, walking toward him.

He shrugged. "Well, I really like lots of different music, but

I always had thing for this song."

"What's it called?"

"*Long Shot.* It's a song from the 80s, but I've been hooked on it ever since I heard it the first time. I think I could listen to it all day and never grow tired of it."

"Guess I'll hafta to listen to it sometime."

He nodded. 'You should. Look it up on your computer and listen. I think you'd like it."

"I might do that."

"You here to check on Bronson?"

"Yes."

"He's doin' fine," he said, putting the brush down. "Come on and take a look."

A few moments later she was looking at the wound, which seemed to be healing quickly. "That looks much better than it did a day or two ago."

"A little TLC goes a long way," he said, smiling. "Kinda like that scratch you got on your elbow when you were a little girl. Mom or Dad kissed it and all of a sudden it wasn't so bad."

She laughed. "Oh, how I remember those days. I was always scratching a knee, an elbow or getting a paper cut. Dad always used to say, 'Don't worry, it'll be better before you're married" and I'd say I wasn't getting married."

He smiled. "I'm sure you will, when the right guy asks."

She shook her head and laughed. "Well, Mr. Right hasn't shown up in my life to ask."

He walked out of the stall and said, "I can't see you bein' like your Mom and marrying somebody shorter than you though. You're about 5 feet 6 inches…"

"Seven."

"Okay, so with heels you'd sneak up close to 5 feet 9, maybe even 5 Feet 10. So, you want some body 6 feet tall or better."

She looked at him and thought, *You're at least 6 feet tall.* A second later she blurted, "I've got to get back to the house."

"Okay. Don't forget to look up that song and listen to it."

A few minutes later Taylor was turning on her computer and looking up the song *Long Shot.* She listened carefully to the words as they were sung and when the song ended, she played it again. A third and a fourth play and she found herself softly singing along.

She got up, walked to the window and saw a half dozen deer slowly making their way toward a stand of Douglas fir trees. When they vanished from view, she picked up her telephone.

Prior to her going to the barn, she'd received a call from a young man she'd dated once. He'd asked if she was free this evening and she eagerly accepted his invitation to dinner. But now she was calling and telling him something had come up and she'd have to cancel.

She sat down on the edge of the bed and stared at her image in the mirror above the nightstand. Taylor wasn't sure how long she stared at her reflection, but she suddenly stood and went back to her computer and once again listened to the song.

She left her room and was headed down the stairs when she caught a glimpse of Jackson through the front door window. He was tossing sticks for the dogs and seemed like he was enjoying himself.

All of a sudden, she felt a very strange and rather cold flutter in her stomach. A moment later she blurted, "No. Oh, no. No, I'm not letting that happen. No. It can't happen."

Later, over dinner, her mother said, "Taylor you seem like you're distracted. Is everything okay?"

"What? Oh… Oh, I'm okay. Just thinking about Christmas gifts for the family."

"You're not waiting till the last minute, again, are you?"

"I might try to get everything done tomorrow."

Then her father joined in. "We hafta start thinkin' about a Christmas tree too."

"Oh, Steven, you're not gonna put another one of those 14 or

15-foot tall trees up again, are you?"

"Now, Rose, there you go tryin' to spoil all the fun for us kids over 20."

"Steven, last year that monstrosity almost toppled over on the grandchildren on Christmas morning."

He shook his head. "Oh, okay, have it your way. But I think we should have at least a 10-footer."

Rose looked at Jackson. "What do you think? Do you agree with Steven?"

"Ma'am, I'm just a guest here, not a member of the family. I really don't believe I should have a say in what the family gets for a Christmas tree."

"Nonsense, Jackson," Mr. Whitfield said. "In fact, I think you and Taylor should choose the tree."

Taylor dropped her spoon into her coffee cup, causing a bit to splash out on to the tablecloth. "What?" she sputtered.

"You and Jackson should go and pick out the tree."

"Dad, I've never chosen the tree. I wouldn't even know what to look for."

He smiled. "That's why I think Jackson should help and it'll be a good experience for both of you."

"Steven, what're you doing?"

"Now, Rose, don't get your feathers ruffled."

"Mr. Whitfield, I consider it an honor that you would even ask me to help pick your family Christmas tree," Jackson said. "If you really want me to do it, sir, I'll gladly help."

"Good. It's settled then. You and Taylor select the Whitfield family Christmas tree."

"Uh, Mr. Whitfield, don't you think you should ask Taylor if that's okay with her?"

He looked over at his daughter and she quickly realized that her father had, for reasons unknown to her, put her on the spot. If she said no, he'd be upset. If she said yes, well that was going to open a door to something entirely new. Although, she was uncertain what that entirely new really was.

"Dad, if it'll make you happy, I'll go with Jackson to pick out a Christmas tree."

At that point Jackson said, "Well, I hope you'll excuse me. I've got to get down to the barn and work on the wagon so it's ready for Friday."

Taylor got up quickly, saying, "And I've got some phone calls to make."

As soon as the kitchen door closed Rose said, "Okay, Steven, what're you up too?"

"Up to? What're you talkin' about?"

"Oh now, Steven, you can't tell me that you aren't trying to push Taylor into caring for Jackson."

"Well, dear, whether you realize it or not, I don't believe for one minute that it's gonna take a whole lotta pushin' to get Taylor to care for Jackson."

"You can't be serious."

"Rose, haven't you noticed that Taylor's seemed preoccupied for the past day or so?"

"Well…"

"And tonight, at dinner, I don't think she said 10 words."

"That certainly doesn't mean she likes or in some way cares about Jackson. My goodness, Steven, he picked her up and threw her in a horse trough."

He grinned. "Yes, he did. And I think that's exactly what she needed."

"You can't mean that."

"Yes, I do mean it. When he tossed her backside in that water trough, it turned her whole world upside down. Nobody ever stood up to her before. Then out of nowhere, a total stranger ignores her orders and sends her into a tizzy and then *splash*. Next, he doesn't apologize to her, although I admit I had a hand in that. So, he does the unthinkable and doesn't apologize."

"Well, why would she care for him after being treated like that?"

"That's exactly why she cares, or at least she's beginning to care. Over the past few years, with all these would be 'Mr. Perfects' she's been screening, not one ever stood up to her and proved he had a backbone. Now..."

"But, Steven..."

'Now, right there in front of her stands Jackson Riley and in her eyes, 'Mr. Imperfect'. Only, Jackson has a set of brass and she's not used to that. 'Mr. Perfect' was an image of what she wanted in her mind. But she's starting to find that her heart has other plans and is reaching out for 'Mr. Imperfect'."

She shook head. "But, the question remains, will the mind or the heart win out?"

"Rose, I hope and pray it's the heart."

"Steven, I just don't understand why you're so... so... Why you see so much in Jackson Riley?"

He nodded. "He's an honest to God, down to earth real man. And, anybody who puts Bob Swanson in his place is solid gold in my eyes."

***

Jackson opened Christmas's stall gate and she followed him to the storage barn. She stood behind him and just to his right as he began touching up a few spots on the old wagon. When he moved to the other side, she followed close on his heels and watched again as he worked to complete his project.

When he was finished, he stepped back and looked over the wagon. He shook his head and said, "Well, girl, I think a couple of Christmas decorations would make it complete. How about you?"

She nodded her head up and down three times and looked on as he attached a Christmas wreath to the tailgate and then affixed two more, one on each side.

He smiled. "Now, that looks like a real Christmas wagon."

"Okay, girl, it's bedtime. Come on."

She walked beside him back into the barn and went straight to her stall without being told. She pulled the gate around until it was closed and looked at Jackson.

"You're not tryin' to pull a fast one on me, are you? I didn't hear the lock click. I bet you were plannin' on sneakin' out to visit your boyfriend."

She rested her chin on the top rail and pulled until the very familiar click sounded.

He grinned, kissed her on the nose and said, "Goodnight, girl. Pleasant dreams."

When he reached the front porch of the house, he began to turn right to go his room when the door opened.

Taylor stepped out and said, "Got a minute?"

"Sure."

"When you finish feeding in the morning, we should stop by the Christmas Store in the mall and pick out some new decorations for the tree and a new wreath for the front door."

"Okay. If that's what you want." He smiled. "I'm yours to command."

She lowered her head and he could see her shivering.

"Get inside before you freeze," he said, putting a hand on her shoulder and opening the door.

She stepped inside, forced a smile and said, "Yes. It is a bit chilly out there."

"Chilly? Yeah, I'd agree that seven degrees is a little on the brisk side."

Another forced smiled. "Okay. It's cold."

"Is something wrong? You don't seem like yourself."

She turned away from his gaze. "I... I just have a lot on my mind."

"Care to talk about it?"

"You wouldn't understand."

"Oh. Why wouldn't I?"

She looked at him and he could see her eyes brimming with tears. "Because I don't understand."

Before he could say a word, she turned and hurried to the stairs. A few moments later he heard her door close and he walked into the kitchen.

He took a beer from the refrigerator, opened it and sat down at the table. He took a sip and said to himself, "Be careful where you tread, Jackson. What you think you see and what you think you feel might be a train wreck waitin' to happen right around the next corner."

Six

Jackson was up and hard at work in the barn before the sun began peeking over the horizon. He fed the horses first, which sent Rooster, Rita, Hank, Sylvester and Sylvia into a yapping, meowing tirade.

"Take a number and get in line," he called to them. "I'll feed you in a few minutes."

Rooster must have been offended by being told to wait his turn. He brazenly grabbed Jackson by the wrist and began tugging, trying his best to pull him back to the dog food container.

Jackson gave him a playful swat on the nose with his glove and said, "Keep it up and you'll be headed to solitary confinement."

Rooster backed away, dropped into a crouch and gave a few shrill yaps, which probably translated to, "Hurry your butt up. I'm starving."

Jackson apparently understood the message and said, "No, you aren't wasting away. In fact, it looks like you should shed a few pounds before Christmas."

He fed Christmas last, but she didn't seem to mind waiting for her breakfast. He patted her softly behind her ears and turned to the chore of calming the dogs and cats.

When they settled down and attacked their breakfast, he took time out to drink some water and wait for the horses to finish their morning grain. He went to Bronson's stall first and checked on his wound and was pleased to see that it was healing nicely.

He began taking the horses out to their pastures and soon only Christmas remained in the barn. He walked into the barn and saw Taylor making her way toward him.

She picked up her pace and was hoping to find a reason to get angry with him. She had decided she was going to force any ideas of romance with Jackson Riley out of her life.

He turned to Christmas and said, "Okay, beautiful..."

"Don't you dare call me beautiful," she shouted.

He immediately fired back, "Hey, don't flatter yourself, I was talkin' to my horse."

A half dozen steps and she was directly in front of him. She stopped and suddenly found she was at a complete loss for words. So, she glared at him and tried to think of something to say.

He looked at her for a moment and then turned to Christmas, saying, "Well, girl, it looks like somebody got outta bed with her mane and forelock on fire."

Taylor blurted, "Are you comparing me to a horse?"

"Only the back end," he replied, wondering why she came in determined to start a fight.

She took another step toward him and glared into his eyes, but again she found no words to hurl back at him.

On the other hand, Jackson was in peek form. "Grouchy this morning, are we? Or, are you lookin' to land the role as the very first female Grinch? But I don't think the color green would do much for your complexion."

She continued trying to hold her icy stare while she searched for a proper and very nasty response.

He looked at the scowl she was struggling to keep and took a chance. He removed his gloves and very gently placed his fingertips at the corners of her mouth.

"Now, if you work hard and turn these upward," he said, as he raised his fingertips, "it'll cause a smile to appear on your face. A very beautiful smile that'll make everyone around you smile."

She glanced down and he grinned. "Ah, yes, I see we have a crack showin' up in Little Miss Grinch's frown." He put his hand under her chin and lifted. "Yes. Yes, we do have a very beautiful smile sneakin' in on the grouch's face."

"Will, you please stop it?" she said, as she looked into his eyes. "Please… just stop it."

"Now, if you're askin' me to stop tryin' to make you laugh or smile, I can't do that. I won't stop."

"Why not," she said, her voice barely a whisper.

Well, here goes, he thought. *Probably about to make a giant fool of myself.* "Whether you take it as a compliment from me or not, when you smile you are an absolutely beautiful woman."

She looked back into his eyes, shook her head and turned away. A moment later she was hurrying for the exit at the far end of the barn.

He opened the stall gate for Christmas. "Well, girl, I guess I really screwed that up."

He walked her to the pasture and as he began closing the gate his phone rang. He looked at the number and answered. "Jackson Riley here. Feeder of horses, dogs and cats and the Court Jester who tried to rescue a Grinch."

There was a brief pause and Taylor said, "I… I'd like to treat the Court Jester to breakfast. Please."

"In spite of my overwhelmingly busy schedule I can be ready in about 45 minutes."

"You'll hafta drive again."

"I'll prepare your carriage, Madam."

Within the hour they were walking into the diner and being led to a booth by, Barb, their waitress. She gave each a menu and said, "Well, are you gonna start the day with another lover's spat?"

Surprisingly, it was Taylor who responded. "Oh, it started first thing this morning.

"My, my. What caused such an early tiff?"

She pointed at Jackson. "He... He compared me to a horse's backside"

Jackson was shocked that Taylor was so easily opening up to Barb, but smiled and shrugged.

"Well, on that note, I'll just leave and get your coffee."

Taylor glanced across the table at Jackson and there it was again, that mischievous little smile. Along with that impish smile she could see a glint in his eyes that said he was probably already planning his next verbal assault.

He picked up his menu, but she continued looking at him. *You have me so confused,* she thought. *I meet you and the first thing you do is throw me in a horse trough. I hated you for that. I hated you for all of a day or so. Then I realize you're not like any man I've ever met and that confused me even more. I keep trying my best to find reasons to hate you and get you out of my life and before I know it, there I am trying to find a reason... any reason to be with you.*

After Barb took their order she said, "When we go to find the Christmas tree, how tall do you think it should be?"

"I kinda like Mr. Whit... your Dad's idea of that 10-footer. It would look great in the center of the room."

She was quiet for a few seconds and then said, "You're right. But I don't like the idea of it being in the center of the room."

He just shrugged and stared at her.

Suddenly, there was a bright glow in her eyes. "It should have lots and lots of lights, red ones and green ones... hundreds and hundreds of them."

He smiled. He liked seeing her glow and hearing the very excited tone in her voice. It was almost as if she'd gone back in time and become a little girl again, anticipating the arrival of Christmas and Santa Claus.

"Oh, I'm just rambling on. I'm sorry."

"No need to apologize. It was fun listening to you. You sounded like you were 8 years old and waiting for Santa to come down the chimney."

"What was it like for you at Christmas time when you were growing up?

Her question caught him off guard and he turned away and looked out the window. Looking back across the table at her he took a deep breath. *I've gotta talk about it sometime. It might as well be now.* Yet, he knew he wouldn't try and tell the whole story.

"Christmas wasn't really a great time in our household. My Dad was a drunk... a very nasty drunk at times. He hated Christmas and he wouldn't allow a Christmas tree in the house or decorations in the windows. Christmas Eve and Christmas Day were very ugly. They could be even uglier the more he had to drink. So, in a nutshell I didn't have an opportunity to enjoy Christmas when I was growing up."

"I'm sorry. I really am."

He tried to force a smile. "You don't hafta be sorry. It wasn't your fault."

Before she could ask another question, breakfast was served and she thought she could ask more about his life later on. Of course, she was still amazed by the breakfast he ordered, but today after he cleaned his plate, he asked Barb for a slice of apple pie with vanilla ice cream... two scoops.

Jackson didn't argue with her when Barb brought the check and quietly got up and walked to the door.

While ringing up the total, Barb said, "Have a very busy day ahead of you?"

"Our first stop is the Christmas store at the mall to pick up new decorations. After that, I'm not sure."

"Well, you two lovebirds have a nice day. And, no fighting in the Christmas store."

Taylor shook her head. "Believe me, we're not an item."

Barb smiled when Taylor handed her a tip and thought, *that's what you think.*

They arrived at the Christmas Store just as the doors were opening. So, being the first customers of the day clearly gave them the advantage of getting a head start on the other shoppers.

Taylor instantly became the perfect image of a little kid in a candy store, gleefully picking out strand after strand of red and green lights. Then came the search for other ornaments, large ones and small ones, and some odd shaped ones.

She turned expecting to see Jackson standing behind her, but saw him talking with a little girl and boy. She watched him drop to one knee as he talked with them and soon, he was magically pulling out a candy cane for each of them.

All of a sudden, Jackson Riley was a magnet for every child in the store. Taylor watched while he talked with each child near him, giving them a candy cane and wishing them a Merry Christmas.

Taylor crossed the store and stood a few feet behind him as he went on talking with the children and handing out candy canes. She saw a woman and a girl she guessed to be about four years old approach him.

She heard the little girl say, "My Daddy's a Marine too."

"Is he here?"

"No, he's away."

He looked up at her mother who said, "He's overseas for a few months."

He nodded, understanding what she meant. "Do you think it would be okay with your Daddy if I gave you a candy cane?"

She looked up at her mother who nodded and she took the candy cane he offered.

Another minute of talking and he knew the little girl's name was Addie and her mother's name was Helen.

Jackson remained on one knee as they talked and Taylor was

stunned over the way he could communicate with her. Yet, she was even more surprised by the way Addie spoke to him.

"My Daddy would always give me a hug every morning and every night."

"That's because he loves you," he said.

"I know. I miss my Daddy's hugs."

Addie moved a little closer. "He told me a secret too. Want to know what it is?"

He smiled and nodded. "If you think it would be okay with your Daddy, you can tell me."

"He said all Marines are brothers."

"Well, that's true. Your Daddy is my brother and I'm his brother."

"I guess it would be okay then." Addie was quiet for a few moments. "Would you give me a hug and I can pretend it's from Daddy?"

Without a word he reached out and put his arms around her. She squeezed tightly for a long moment and finally stepped back. She paused, leaned forward him kissed him on the cheek.

She looked at him again and moved closer, whispering in his ear. "My eyes got wet."

"That's okay," he said. "Sometimes mine get wet too."

Her mother buried her face in her hands and wept as Taylor spun around and hurried to the back of the store. Jackson stood up with Addie in his arms and a second later Helen put her head on his shoulder and cried.

***

It was lunchtime when Jackson and Taylor carried packages through the front door. Steve and Rose were home and preparing to have lunch and hoped they'd join them. Taylor declined and went to her room, but Jackson dined with them and talked about working with Christmas during the early afternoon.

When he left to go to the barn, Taylor came into the kitchen and sat down at the table. It was obvious to her parents that she was troubled over something and asked if they could help.

She took a deep breath. "I don't even know where to begin. But, at breakfast this morning, Jackson opened up a little about his childhood and I was shocked. He..."

Once she began, the story of the morning's events flowed out easily. That is until she began telling them of Jackson and the little girl in the Christmas Store. She tried to chock back the tears, but it was no use. It took a while, but she was at last able to relate what he'd done.

By now her mother was also crying and shaking her head and her father took a breath and swallowed the lump in his throat. When everyone regained their composure, her father appeared to be lost in his thoughts.

"I think I've known since the day I first met Jackson that he didn't have the best life growing up," he said. "There was, and still is, something about him that says there's a lotta pain in his heart. I don't know what it is and I'm certain he won't open up to anybody about it until he's ready to talk. And, I don't believe he'll talk to just anyone. He's gonna hafta to completely trust them."

Taylor wiped at her eyes. "I can't imagine what it must've been like never having a Christmas tree or decorations of any kind in your house at Christmas."

Her father nodded. "When he told me he'd had eight years of military school, I suspected there was much more behind that. I just didn't feel it was my place to try and dig deeper into his personal life."

Taylor looked at him and said, "Do you really think he'll ever open up and tell somebody about his past?"

Her father was silent for a few moments. "I don't know. I see some things, or at least I think I see some things that says he'd like to tell someone... when the time's right. But the time and who he tells is up to him."

"I guess you're right.

"Now, why don't we put ourselves back together and go to the barn," he said, pushing his chair back. "I'd like to go see what Jackson's doing." He laughed. "Probably teachin' Christmas to put her saddle on."

They arrived at the indoor arena about 30 minutes later and saw Jackson sitting on Christmas and taking a slow walk around the paddock. He was riding without a saddle and the reins were crossed and draped over her at the withers.

They watched him reach out and gently tap her twice on the left side of her neck. Immediately she turned to her left and kept up the slow pace. Moments later he gently tapped her on the right side of her neck and she turned to the right. After a leisurely walk he called "Whoa" and she stopped. A second later he reached behind and tapped her twice gently on the back. Immediately she began to back up. When she stopped, he slid off her back and dropped to the soft floor of the arena.

He walked toward the trio with Christmas by his right side. "Hello, Mr. Whitfield, Mrs. Whitfield." He turned to Taylor, took off his black Cowboy hat and said. "And good afternoon to you, Ma'am. A pleasure to see you... I think."

She shook her head and tried to hide her smile, but it was no use. "I swear you're like a... a wayward child."

He gave her a low bow, sweeping his hat across the front of his body. "Why thank you, Ma'am. Coming from you, I take that as a compliment."

"Jackson, how'd you teach your horse those tricks?" Steve said.

"Well, sir, they're not exactly tricks. I just wondered if I could get her to respond to a tap instead of a voice, leg or rein command. I started by givin' her the verbal commands and each time I did, I gave her a tap... actually two. I kept that up and finally tried it without the voice commands and, like magic, she responded."

Steve smiled. "Son, I've believed from the first time I saw you two together, she'd do anything for you. You two were meant for each other."

"Could you teach Bronson to respond like that?" Taylor said.

"Why don't you train Bronson?"

"Oh, I don't think I could do that."

"Sure you can. Let's get your horse and start."

Before she could object, he took the bridle off Christmas and began walking toward the barn. As always, she was by his right side and keeping pace with him.

This being the first time Rose had the opportunity to see his horse in action, she was in awe. But when she watched her go into stall and close the gate she shook her head in disbelief.

"That's the most amazing thing I've ever seen," she gushed.

He smiled. "Well, Ma'am, I still haven't been able to teach her to cook."

Taylor said, "I'll get Bronson saddled and…"

"You don't need a saddle."

"But I've always been afraid to ride bareback."

He shrugged. "Well then, we'll just hafta make this a trainin' session for two. Take him in there and lunge him and burn off some energy and we'll go from there."

Twenty minutes later, Taylor was mounted on her horse and ready to take her first ride without a saddle.

"What happens if I fall off?"

"I'm right here. I'll catch you."

"But what if I fall off on the other side?"

He laughed. "Well then you'd better hope you land on your backside."

"Are you saying I have a big backside?" she shrieked.

"I did not say that. I just said you better hope you fall on your backside. It's better then fallin' on your head. Besides, if you fall on your head, you'll probably damage the floor of the arena."

"I'm gonna ignore that comment," she said. "Now, can we start the lesson, please?"

"Okay. But, we're only gonna work on one part at a time. We'll start with backin' up. I think that's the easiest."

On the sidelines, Rose turned to her husband. "Steven, how long has this been going on?

"How long's what been goin' on?"

"This bantering back and forth."

He grinned. "I believe it started the day they met."

"You know, as much as I hate to admit it, I think she really likes this young man.

"Rose, I think it might be a step or two beyond the she like's him stage."

"Steven, you can't mean that."

"We've had somewhat of a similar discussion earlier. Right now, Taylor's in a battle with what she'd planned as the dream life for herself and movie star Mr. Perfect and Jackson, who is the exact opposite of the man in her fantasy life."

"I noticed that his bantering with her seems kind of, oh I guess lighthearted and maybe even funny. I wonder why?"

"My opinion… lighthearted and funny can go a long way in easing or even hiding pain."

Seven

While the training session continued, Steve and Rose slipped quietly from the arena and returned to the house. As they walked in, the telephone began ringing and Steve answered by the third ring.

It was Helen Davidson. "I'm trying to get in touch with a Jackson Riley and I was told I could probably reach him at your residence."

"He's here, but at the barn at the present."

"Would you give him a message for me?

"Yes, Ma'am, I certainly will."

"I'd like to know if he can stop by this evening if he's free. I have a Face-time call set up with my husband and I'd like him to be able to thank Jackson for what he did for Addie this morning."

"If you'll give me your phone number, I'll have him call as soon as he comes in."

It wasn't long afterward that he saw Jackson and Taylor on their way to the house. He certainly wasn't aware of the topic, but he guessed it to be another of their verbal jousting matches.

"Are you sure you weren't insinuating that my backside was too big?"

He laughed. "Taylor, I never said or insinuated anything like that."

"Yes, you did."

"Look, if I had said something like. 'If you land on your butt, you'll probably bounce 60 feet in the air," you could take that as an insult to the size of your backside. Or, if I'd said something along the lines of you should hang warning flags from your back pockets, then you'd have a right to yell and scream. But, I didn't."

She slowed her pace and feigned tying her boot, allowing him to get several feet in front of her. He paused and looked over his shoulder in time to see the snowball hurtling toward him. He stepped to his left, but it still glanced off his shoulder.

"That's for lying," she yelled.

"You're beggin' for another dip in the horse trough."

He turned toward the house and noticed the truck slowly coming down the driveway. A second later and he saw the TV News logo on the side of the truck. Suddenly, he had that old, very familiar uneasy feeling in the pit of his stomach.

By the time he and Taylor reached the front porch one of the men was out of the truck.

"I'm looking for Jackson Riley."

He was about to respond that Jackson wasn't there when a woman came from the other side of the truck. "Mr. Riley, we'd like to have a few minutes of your time."

Although he was sure he knew why they were there, he said, "May I ask what this is about?"

"Mr. Riley, we've had a half-dozen people send videos to the station of you and a young girl in the Christmas Store this morning. That was such a heartwarming thing you did and we would like our viewing audience to see what a wonderful thing you did."

"I didn't do anything special. I…"

"Mr. Riley, two people captured the entire event on film. It is something quite remarkable and especially at this time of year."

"Look, I did something for a little girl because her father can't be here to give her a hug. But, more than that, I did it for a brother. If the roles were reversed, he would've done exactly the same for me."

"I'm sure of that, but we'd still like to hear more from you."

"You have the film that was sent to your station and I know you recorded what we've said here. That should be enough for now."

"Would you consider an interview at a later time?"

"No. Absolutely not."

When they returned to their truck, Taylor said, "You really should've given them an interview."

"I don't think it was that newsworthy."

She stepped directly in front of him. "You don't really have any idea what you did, do you? Every person in that store cried over what you did for that little girl... including me. Jackson, they cried for a good and very beautiful thing. Tonight, when that story airs, as short as it may be, hundreds more people are gonna cry."

He turned and looked away from her gaze for a moment and then said, "They wanna make the story about me. It should be about Addie and her mother. Tell people about a little girl who misses her father, his hugs and bedtime stories and a wife and mother who has to face an uncertain fear every time there's a knock at the door or the phone rings. That's the real story. I just happened to come along at a time when a little girl named Addie missed her father so much she was willing to take a hug from a stranger. I..."

"She didn't see you as a stranger. She saw you as her father's brother, just as he'd told her. That made what you did special to her and her mother."

"But I want the story they tell to be about Addie and her mother, not me."

"Well, you've convinced me. I'll call the TV station and tell them to make the story about Addie and her mother. Will that satisfy you?"

She surprised him, but he said, "Yes, it would. Thank you.

She stepped a little closer. "I believe there's something else, something you don't want people to know. A secret you've kept, probably for most of your life and you're afraid to let anyone in to see it."

"Really? What's that?"

"You're afraid somebody might see past your ice-cold suit of Marine armor. Go ahead and keep playing that tough, hard Marine, but I know what's hiding behind your nasty stare and snarl. I know there's a warm and caring heart and so does Addie, as well as that beautiful Buckskin Mare you rescued. You just don't want people to know, because that would mean letting them get close you. I don't know why you put that barrier there, but only you can open the door."

She turned, walked into the house and began calling the area TV stations. In no time at all, Taylor proved she was excellent at presenting a strong case for Addie and Helen to be the topic of their story.

Steve gave Jackson the message from Helen Davidson and he called to confirm he would be there by eight o'clock. He returned to the barn immediately and began preparing hay and grain buckets for the evening feeding. Then he moved on to the next chore, cleaning and filling the water buckets.

By the time he brought Christmas in it was dark and the air temperature was dropping rapidly.

"Okay, girl, get in your house and stay warm."

He smiled as she casually walked into her stall and turned to close the gate. She backed up a step and continued looking at him, waiting for her goodnight kiss.

"You think you're pretty slick. You closed your gate, but you didn't lock it."

She rested her chin on the top rail, pulled and the lock closed. Now, he went to her and gave her a kiss on the nose. As he stepped back, she gave a whinny and a second later Bronson responded.

He laughed. "Tellin' your boyfriend you won't be able to

sneak out for a clandestine rendezvous?" He reached in his pocket, pulled out a piece of carrot and gave it to her. "Don't worry, I'll give one to your lover on the way out."

He hurried to the house, showered and dressed for dinner. A casual walk down the hallway and he went into the kitchen. There he found Taylor and her mother talking and tried to leave.

Taylor said, "You don't hafta go. Grab a beer and sit down."

He took a bottle of Coors from the refrigerator and sat down at the table. He was about to say something, but Rose began talking again with Taylor.

"Okay, you've finally decided what you want to do with your company."

Taylor nodded. "Yes, I'm definitely selling and moving back here. I've been offered far more than I was about to ask and I stand to make a very substantial profit."

"Are you planning to reopen here?

"Yes. That was my plan all along. At first, I thought about a space at the mall, but the rental fees are outrageous. There are three spaces available on the main street through town and one of those is perfect."

Her mother shook her head and said, "Taylor, are you sure about opening your store along the main street? I would think you'd attract far more customers at the mall."

"I thought so too… at first. But then I realized we have lots of traffic through Cedar Falls year-round. If they shop, the majority would shop right along the main street because it's convenient. And I've already checked with other shop owners and their businesses thrive the entire year and mostly because of the shoppers who were just passing through."

"Well, I still think the mall would be the better choice."

Before Taylor could answer, Jackson said, "Ma'am I agree with what Taylor said. In just the short time I've been here, I've noticed the volume of traffic, both cars and pedestrians along the main street. Sid, the barbershop owner, said he gets a steady stream of out of town customers every week."

Rose nodded. "Okay. When do you plan to make the move?"

"It would be sometime after the first of the year. It'll take a few weeks to get everything finalized and then I'll get everything organized here and hopefully, I'll have my store open by March."

"What type of business do you own," Jackson said.

"I have a women's clothing store where I offer a wide variety of women's wear from less expensive to top of the line. But I offer everything at a reasonable price and it keeps the customers happy and coming back."

"What's the name of your store?"

"My Roommate's Closet."

"I like that." He smiled. "In fact, the name alone would be enough to make me wanna come in and look around."

She nodded. "That's the idea."

***

Jackson asked Taylor to accompany him and they arrived at the Davidson residence shortly before eight. Addie immediately took Jackson by the hand and was doing her best to drag him down the hallway to the computer.

"Addie, please don't yank on Mr. Riley's arm."

"Ma'am, please call me Jackson."

"That's fine for me, but I don't want Addie calling you by your first name."

"Oh, I understand that, Ma'am."

Helen laughed. "And please… you don't hafta call me Ma'am."

"Sorry. Force of habit and one habit that I'll probably never break."

Addie began calling to them telling them to hurry because Daddy was there.

Jackson and Taylor stood in the background while Helen and

Addie told of their meeting Jackson in the mall and how he'd been so kind to them. He too seemed overwhelmed by what Jackson had done and, after swallowing a lump or two in his throat, offered his thanks.

"No need to thank me, Gunny. I did it for a brother."

"Well, thank you anyway."

They spoke for a few more minutes and Jackson learned that Gunnery Sergeant Wyatt Davidson was just one in a long line of family members who were Marines.

Finally, Jackson said, "Gunny, let me put your family back on."

"Thanks again. Semper Fi, brother."

"Oooh Rah. Stay safe, brother."

When they were preparing to leave, Taylor invited Helen and Addie to the Whitfield farm for Friday night's wagon ride event.

Helen happily accepted, saying, "Thank you so much. But now I'm sure Addie won't sleep just thinking about it."

While they were walking to his truck, Jackson said, "I think your father's really excited about the wagon ride idea. In fact, he said he wants to be the 'Wagon Master'."

"That's sure gonna break Diane's heart."

"Why."

"She was counting on you being the 'Wagon Master' so she could ride up there beside you." She laughed. "She has a crush on you and I'm sure she's hoping to snuggle up to you on the wagon."

He grinned. "I'll let her down gently."

She shook her head and smiled. "Oh, I'm sure you will."

There was sudden silence that filled the cab of the truck and the seconds slowly ticked by and then he said, "You're right, you know."

"About what?"

"The barrier."

She turned and looked at him. "Why put up a barrier? It just keeps people away."

"If you don't let people get too close, they can't hurt you."

"You mean they can't break your heart, right?"

"That's part of it." He was quiet again for a few moments. "I guess there was way too much pain and heartbreak early on and I didn't wanna deal with it anymore."

"Oh, come on. Don't tell me you've never been in love or had a girlfriend."

A few seconds passed and he smiled. "Well, back in high school I was in love with a girl named Jenny."

A moment later he was telling Taylor of his first real love.

"My military academy was a mile away from an all girls school and the principals decided it would be a good idea to have monthly gatherings. Then, it became every two weeks. The idea was to have dances and they soon found that thought was a disaster. The boys couldn't dance or refused to dance, so they decided to fix that problem. Before we knew it, there were mandatory dance classes for a half-hour a day, five days a week. I was in the sixth grade when this happened and, as I guess you'd expect, us boys weren't exactly thrilled with the idea.

"Well, like it or not, I was learning and by my junior year of high school I was actually a very good dancer."

"You're a good dancer!"

"Believe it or not, yes. But, I'm probably a little on the rusty side now. It's been a while since I was on a dance floor."

"There's a dance next Saturday night at St. Martin's Church. You've just gotta go. My mom loves to dance. What dances do you know?" She was firing questions faster. "Would you dance with my mother? She'd love it."

"Okay. Okay, one thing at a time." He glanced over at her and noticed the bright smile on her face. "As far as dances... and again, this is a believe it or not, our dance lessons included waltz, jitterbug, cha-cha, square dancing and even ballroom dancing."

"Really?" she blurted. "You know how to ballroom dance?"
He shook his head. "Yes, I do."

"I can't believe it. Mom loves ballroom dancing, but it's not exactly dad's favorite. In fact, he's horrible at it." She reached over and touched his arm. "Please go. Go and dance with mom."

"Are you going?"

"Yes."

"Good. I didn't wanna show up with your mother and have a town rumor started."

She laughed. "Okay. Back to Jenny."

"Jenny didn't show up at the school until her junior year. At the very first dance of the new school year she latched on to me the instant the music started. That was it. From then on it was Jenny and me and no one could pry us apart. Naturally, that ruffled a few egos because Jenny was one of the pretties girls there and a few guys took offense to our relationship."

"Did that cause any big problems?"

"Let's just say none that I couldn't handle and leave it at that." He shrugged and went on. "Sometime in late October, Jenny introduced me to her parents. They were cordial at first, then the bomb fell and they told her to stay away from me and me to stay away from her. Well, with that ultimatum in place, it cemented our relationship until graduation."

"What happened after graduation?"

"Her family moved to Oregon and Jenny went with them. At first, we talked a few days a week and even talked about tryin' to get together. Near the end of summer, I was the only one makin' the calls and then, for whatever reason, she stopped answering my calls. I figured she found a new boyfriend and I decided very quickly that I didn't especially enjoy the whole process of mending a broken heart. So, up went the barrier. But, to be honest, I think the barrier was in place long before that. I just let my guard down and walked right in for punch to the heart."

"You mean you were never involved in a serious relationship after Jenny?"

He shrugged. "No. I was strictly hit and run. I made it clear from the beginning, I wasn't interested in a permanent relationship and if that's what they were lookin' for, they certainly had the wrong guy?"

She was quiet for a few moments. "Do you think you'll ever change?"

He looked over at her. "If the right woman comes along, I'm sure I could open the door and let her in."

She almost asked who or what type of woman would be the right one. She glanced out the window and thought, *I sure hope you change soon. Oh, my God! What in the world am I thinking? Why am I even thinking something like this?*

Later that night Taylor turned on her computer and was soon listening to *Long Shot* once again. Then, as Jackson had said she was finding the song almost addicting and it seemed to beckon her to listen again and again.

While listening to the song for the third time, she wrapped her arms around her pillow. Seconds later, tears trickled from the corners of her eyes and she whispered, "Oh, I'm so confused right now. Jackson can't be my long shot at love… can he?"

Eight

While Taylor fought with her emotions, Jackson was in the storage barn unleashing a relentless attack on the heavy bag. In the midst of his unrelenting pummeling of the bag he began emitting what could only be described as a growl as each punch landed.

When he ended his savage beating, he muttered, "Wake up, Jackson. You're opening the door. If you let her squeeze in, you could end up regretting it."

He walked round and round the barn, trying to cool his fury as much as his body. He was uncertain how long he'd paced, but he picked up his shirt and jacket and walked to the barn.

Christmas was at the stall gate when he entered almost as if she'd known he was coming to visit. She nodded her head up and down and gave a soft nicker as he drew near. He kissed her on the nose, placed his hands on the sides of her head and kissed her again, this time between the eyes.

He ran his hand gently up and down her face, saying, "I'm so blessed to have you." He smiled. "You listen to all my troubles and never ask for anything in return. Right now, I've got another worry beginnin' to sneak up on me.

"Yeah, it's that very beautiful, blue eyed blonde I tossed in the horse trough. At first, I wasn't too sure about her. I guess I thought she was just some stuck-up little snob who I wouldn't want to be around. Then before you know it, there we are goin' places together and I kinda started likin' her company, but I'm not gonna tell her."

He pulled a peppermint treat from his pocket and gave it to Christmas. "There's all kinds of things goin' on around here now. I guess that's because it's so close to Christmas. I see the kids in town and they're all laughin' and you feel their excitement if you get close to them.

"I never knew what that was like when I was their age. I sure wonder every now and then what it would've been like if Dad didn't drink and tell Mom and me, we weren't gonna celebrate Christmas. He wouldn't even let us go to church."

He gave her another peppermint treat and took a deep breath. "I go to church sometimes, but I should probably find a church and go every Sunday. I know I wanna go to church on Christmas Eve and listen to the choir and I guess just be there to see what it's like.

"Another thing I've gotta do is find my mother and I'm gonna start tomorrow just as soon as I've finished my chores here. We need to find each other. If we do that, I think it would be a good start to a whole new side of life.

"I'd like her to meet Taylor. I'm sure she'd..." He stopped and very slowly shook his head. "What am I sayin'? And... and why'd I say it?"

He gave Christmas another kiss and said, "Goodnight my beautiful princess. I'll see you in the morning."

Jackson turned out the lights, stepped outside into the cold night air and closed the barn door behind him. He walked toward the house at a very slow, deliberate pace.

He exhaled and his breath became a misty white cloud that vanished on the wings of a soft breeze. The stars, that seemed like countless millions shone brightly in the clear night sky, while the call of an owl broke the nocturnal silence.

Off to his right, an endless array of oak, walnut and elm trees stood silent, their barren limbs reaching upward as if hoping to touch a star. On his left, the pine, cedar and fir trees still held their year round green and seemed as though they wanted to shade the snow with a blanket of majestic emerald.

He was halfway to house when he felt the eyes. They were there looking at him as he walked and, somehow he knew Taylor was watching from a window. For a fleeting instant he wished she'd meet him at the door.

Sometime later in rooms not so far apart, in the hazy clouds of dreamland two worlds clashed and went their separate ways.

***

Jackson was completing his morning feeding duties when Steve Whitfield rushed into the barn. He was a man filled with new ideas and wanted to share them with Jackson over breakfast. In the blink of an eye Steve disappeared after telling Jackson to get Taylor and meet him at the diner.

Taylor was already waiting for him when he returned to the house. "Dad's got some kind of wild idea about Friday night and wants us to be a part of it."

He laughed. "Well, I'd like to grab a quick shower. I don't really wanna go to breakfast smelling like the barn."

"Good idea. You don't want people confusing you with the back end of a horse."

He stopped in his tracks, looked at her and smiled. "Okay. Put that one in your corner. You got me."

"Two can play your game, Mr. Riley."

"Now, that sounds like a challenge."

"Take it any way you want. But hurry and get that shower before we hafta air out the house."

"Wow! What fired you up this morning?"

Her only response was a very mischievous smile and he had to admit he was looking forward to whatever was ahead with this unexpected side of Taylor.

They arrived at the diner and found Steve sipping a coffee and talking with Barb.

When they sat down, she looked at them and said, "And what are the lovebirds battling over this morning?"

Taylor tried to respond, but Jackson beat her to it. "Well, she referred to me as the back end of a horse."

"I'm sure you deserved it."

"Oh, he did," Taylor said.

"Wait a minute, this is two against one. You're ganging up on me."

Barb turned and began walking away. "I'll be back with your coffee."

Steve looked from Taylor to Jackson and, for a moment, was about to ask what was going on, but decided against it. Instead he said, "I'd really like to do a lot more for the kids on Friday and I wanna include Helen Davidson and Addie. I'd like to talk with Helen and have her get in touch with all the military families she knows who live in the area and invite them. Are you okay with that?"

Jackson nodded. "You're hosting the party. Do what you think's best."

"I agree with Jackson."

"Good." He took a sip of his coffee and went on. "I think we should have a bonfire and have the kids and their parents roast hotdogs over the fire. We can have hot chocolate, juices and water to drink. You know, a little warm-up before the wagon ride."

"Dad, won't we need somebody else to help with this?"

"I've already taken care of that."

Jackson laughed. "It sounds like you've had this all planned out."

"Well, actually it was a spur of the moment idea. But it fell together pretty quick."

"Who's gonna help," Taylor said.

"I talked with Juanita and she's sure she can get her sister and two cousins to help. Then I spoke with Jose and George and they're all for it."

Jackson grinned. "What did you do? Call everybody in the middle of the night?"

"Oh, no. I got the ball rollin' last evening while you were over at the Davidson's."

"Dad, if everything comes together the way you want, will one wagon be enough?"

"I've taken care of that too. I spoke with Pete Wells and he's gonna hook up his wagon and join in." He smiled. "With him right there across from us, he won't have far to travel."

Barb arrived with coffee for Taylor and Jackson. She took their orders, asking Taylor first and then Steve Whitfield. Then she turned to Jackson and said, "Your usual, Sir?"

"Yes, Ma'am. That's just fine."

"I'll have the cook roll the dumpster out."

Taylor burst out laughing, while Jackson stared at Barb and said, "What is this? Taylor starts first thing this morning and now you jump on the 'let's get Jackson' train."

Steve looked from Barb to Taylor to Jackson and said, "I'm apparently missing something."

"Only Jackson's appetite, Dad. If you think he eats a lot at dinner, wait 'til you see breakfast."

The banter settled and the discussion turned back to Friday and preparing for the evening. It was decided that Jackson and Taylor would be the designated shoppers and they should start as soon as breakfast was over.

Jackson nodded in agreement, but knew that would delay his intended search for his mother. But, at the present time, he didn't want to bother anyone else with his problem. He'd begin when he and Taylor completed shopping for groceries.

With breakfast out of the way Jackson and Taylor were soon walking around the Cedar Falls Food Mart and filling their grocery cart. They picked up hotdog rolls, mustard, ketchup, sweet and dill relish, marshmallows and hot chocolate mix. Next came napkins, plastic knives, forks, spoons, paper plates and finally the beverages. The hotdogs would be purchased from the Cedar Falls Meat and Poultry Company.

When they began the drive home, Jackson said, "Friday night we should saddle our horses and ride along with the wagons."

She glanced over and said, "Yes. Yes. Why not? That could be lots of fun."

"Good, and I'll decorate Bronson and Christmas."

"Okay. How are you gonna decorate the horses?"

"I'd rather surprise you."

She looked at him and thought, "*You've already surprised me and in more ways than you can imagine. You've thrown my entire dream of the perfect life completely off track. I wanted to hate you for that. I tried to hate you but...*"

"Okay. Time to unload the groceries."

"What? How'd we get home so fast?"

"I ordered up Warp Drive."

"Okay, Captain Kirk, let's unload the truck."

It took close to twenty minutes to unload the truck and get everything organized. Then Jackson said he had some work to do and went to his room.

He considered his initial idea in the search for his mother might be a waste of time but thought he'd try anyway. He located a telephone number for his Uncle Bill and dialed the number.

His call was answered on the third ring and as soon as he identified himself, all hell broke loose. His Uncle Bill cursed him and told him he had no idea where his mother was and ended the conversation by saying that if he did know, he wouldn't reveal her location to Jackson.

For his part, Jackson unleashed a volley of expletives on his uncle and ended by thinking how much he'd love to strangle him.

After he calmed down, he began a lengthy computer search using her maiden name, Mary Barton. After a while, he wondered how so many women named Mary Barton could be in one area. A search of over two hours left him frustrated and asking himself if he'd ever find her.

He walked out to the pasture and brought Christmas in and began to groom her. He paused, gave her an apple treat and said, "Don't forget, Gary's coming by in the morning to give you a nice manicure and fit you with new shoes." He laughed. "But you're not getting high heels."

He slowly brushed her forelock, mane and tail and then chose another brush for her coat. He lost all track of time as he seemed to do whenever he was with Christmas.

Just as he finished brushing her, Steve Whitfield came in and said, "Taylor told me you managed to get everything on the grocery list."

"Yes, Sir. Shopping went off without a hitch." He reached into his pocket. "I forgot to give your credit card back to Taylor."

He smiled. "Well, I'm sure I could trust you not to max it out."

On the spur of the moment he told Steve of his search for his mother. Without hesitation, Steve offered his assistance and said he'd be willing to do whatever was necessary to help him in his quest.

Jackson thanked him and asked that he keep everything they discussed regarding his mother confidential.

A nod and a pat on the back was all the assurance necessary as Steve turned and headed outside to the pasture.

Nine

Over dinner Jackson said, "Mr. Whitfield, how did your draft horses get the names Comet and Cupid?"

"Well, my grandson, Josh, gave them their names," he said with a big smile. "I think he was four at the time and I'd just read him Twas The Night Before Christmas for about the tenth time that day. Later, when I said I was going to the barn, he wanted to go with me."

"Steven, as I recall, you whispered in Josh's ear and all of a sudden he's saying 'Grandpa, let's go to the barn'."

"Now, Rose, I don't remember it like that."

"Oh, now you have a memory lapse."

He smiled. "Well, regardless, Josh and I went on down to the barn and I told him that Santa Claus could borrow the draft horses on Christmas Eve if he needed them. Out of the blue, Josh grabs me by the arm and says we should name them Comet and Cupid so Santa would know they were for him if he needed them."

Jackson laughed. "It makes perfect sense to me."

"They've been Comet and Cupid ever since."

"Will Josh and Anna be here for the bonfire and wagon ride, Mr. Whitfield?"

"I spoke to Andrew this morning and he said he, Beth and the kids would be here early Friday afternoon."

"I'm sure they'll enjoy themselves."

A few minutes later, Jackson excused himself, saying he wanted to check over the wagon again to be certain it was ready for Friday.

Soon, he was walking around the wagon looking it over with Christmas by his side. Each time he paused to look something over, she rested her chin on his shoulder as though assisting him with his inspection. So, he'd pause in his inspection tour long enough to give her a gentle scratching on her nose.

When he took Christmas back to the barn, he found the dogs and cats seated in front of the tack room. Immediately there came a chorus of meows and soft woofs, which surely indicated they were waiting for Jackson's attention.

He shook his head, smiled and looked at Christmas. "Okay, girl, go to your house."

When she closed her stall door, Rooster and Rita dropped to the floor and rolled on to their backs. A few moments later they were showing their approval for the tummy rub with a series of grunts and an occasional head roll from one side to the other.

Next, came time for back scratches for the cats. This task offered its own dilemma of three cats and only two hands. And, all three expected to have their back scratched at the same time. With one having to wait there was always an unusual amount of hissing, back arching, spitting and growling. Occasionally, a swatting match ensued meaning Jackson would surely receive a few scratches on his hands while trying to ward off an all-out feline war.

Sometimes when feline tensions were bordering on a full blown battle, Christmas would whinny. Bronson would answer and in only a matter of seconds all horses were adding their voices to the chorus. Naturally, this inspired Rooster and Rita to add their voices with shrill yapping or a bit of hearty barking.

Tonight, the combination of horses whinnying, dogs barking

and cats hissing and spitting, brought Steve and Taylor rushing from the house.

When they opened the door at the far end of the barn and stepped inside, Jackson stood up and called out, "Okay, boys and girls, that's enough."

The old adage "Fat Chance" suddenly came to mind when the din grew louder. But, two additional parties joined in, adding their laughter to the ruckus.

Jackson threw his hands up in surrender and yelled, "Who started this?"

"I bet you did," Taylor shouted while walking toward him.

It took time to restore order to the barn and it took a full five minute "black out" to finally end the pandemonium. When Taylor turned the lights back on it was so quiet the silence felt odd.

She noticed the scratches on the backs of Jackson's hands and said, "You'd better let me clean those up."

When she took him by the arm and began leading him to the tack room and the first aid kit, Steve smiled and slipped unnoticed from the barn.

She opened the first aid kit and removed an alcohol swab packet. She tore open the packet and touched the swab to the back of his hand. When he didn't flinch, she shook her head, looked into his eyes and said, "Mean and tough no matter what."

He didn't respond, so she continued. "You know, I can't help but wonder what you'd be like if you opened the door and tore down that barrier you've built around your heart."

"Does it really matter that much to you?"

Without thinking she said, "Yes."

"Why?"

"Well, what I meant was… I… I think it would be a good thing for you and everyone around you."

"Oh. For a few seconds I thought you might've meant…"

"No," she blurted, shaking her head. "Don't try and read too much into what I said."

He smiled. "I'll try my best to remember that."

They left the barn together and began the walk to the house. Suddenly, he took her by the arm and stopped.

"What's wrong?"

"Nothing," he said. "I just thought you might like to stop and enjoy everything around you. There's so much here to appreciate. I mean, just look at what's here. Look up in the sky and there're so many stars on a clear night like this. Millions. And they're all there for you."

He swept his hand in a wide arc. "And look around you at this. Look at the trees, the snow covering the ground and think of the dozens of animals out there watching you right now. And all of it... everything is there for you."

"I don't believe you. I mean you're amazing. I've lived here my entire life and I didn't see any of this until you showed me. How did you... How can you see what I missed?"

He glanced up into the night sky and around at the trees. "I didn't always see it. I found it when I learned how precious life is. The sad thing is far too many people die without ever knowing or seeing the gifts that were there for them."

"Thank you."

"For what?"

"Opening my eyes."

"You can return the favor when you help someone open their eyes."

She turned, reached out and took his hand and they walked in silence to the house. There a quick goodnight and they went off with their own thoughts of what tonight might bring for tomorrow.

***

Jackson was out bright and early the next morning... Friday morning. He drove into Cedar Falls to pick up pastries and coffee for Jose and George.

He was happy this morning, knowing what was ahead for Friday evening. He felt it would be a special evening for the kids and he couldn't wait to be a part of it.

Before he knew it, Jose and George had cleaned the stalls and left for their next job. He had kept Christmas inside and headed for her stall to get her out for grooming.

He started, as always, with a kiss on her nose and then the ritual of combing and brushing. This morning Sylvia dropped by and sat down to observe what was going on. After a minute or so, Christmas lowered her head and gave the cat a very gentle nudge. Sylvia responded by standing on her hind legs and extending her body upward as far as possible. She was able to rest her paws just below the horse's right ear and it looked as if she was sharing a secret with her.

Jackson smiled. "I see you've found yourself another friend. That's good."

He stopped for a moment and watched the interaction-taking place between horse and cat. Sylvia purred and rubbed her head up and down the right side of Christmas's face for a time before turning and going back to her food dish.

Jackson patted Christmas on the neck. "You know, girl, the journey through life can be a long and lonely walk without family or friends.

"When I was growin' up that walk sure seemed longer and far more lonely than I was ready for. It took a while for me to get used to my world without a family. I'm sure that was because of seein' all the other boys and girls my age with their parents. I always kinda envied them, but later on I found out that some of them didn't have the best lives either. But I really only knew about my pain and I never shared that secret with anybody. That's because of that wall I put up between me and everybody else."

He rubbed her softly under the chin and said, "Right now I'm a little mixed up in my feelings. Sometimes I feel like I wanna talk with Taylor and tell her my secrets, but then I'm not sure if I should. I'm startin' to really enjoy her company and, I confess, that scares me and I know that's only because I don't wanna get hurt."

He kissed her on the nose. "I know I can share any secret with you and it's safe. And, I know I'll never be without a good friend as long as I have you in my life."

At that instant she took a bite of the chocolate chip cookie he was holding in his left hand.

He shook his head and laughed. "Okay, Pogey Bait Queen, I guess that's your reward for being my friend and therapist. I'm sure Sergeant Reckless is smilin' down on you right now and she's proud of you."

He opened the barn door and said, "Come on. Time to go to the pasture." She walked beside him and tried to sneak another bite of his cookie. "Well, sometime I'm gonna tell you all about Sergeant Reckless. She was a horse, but not just any horse. She was a Marine during the Korean War and a hero. Then you'll know all about the very first Pogey Bait Queen and what a great Marine she was."

***

Today was also the day chosen by Helen Davidson to give her interview to the press. By 10:00 AM, the TV and newspaper reporters had squeezed into her living room, anxious to hear her story.

Addie was seated on the sofa by her side as she told them how difficult it was with her husband overseas and having to be a single parent until his return.

"With Christmas coming, it's even more difficult without Wyatt and that's especially true since Addie was born. He's such a proud and loving father and it's so tough for Addie because he's not always here to tell her those bedtime stories and kiss her goodnight. But at this time of year, his absence takes more of a toll on both of us emotionally."

She went on with her story and told of meeting Jackson at the mall and what an impact he had on Addie.

"More than anything, Addie wanted a big hug from her father and it was getting more and more difficult with each passing day trying to explain that Daddy can't come home. When we went into the Christmas Store, the thought of her father being away was about to overwhelm her. Then there he was. I don't know how or why, but Jackson Riley just seemed to appear out of nowhere. When Addie saw the Marine logo on his sweatshirt, that was all it took."

She continued telling them about their meeting and the hug he gave Addie and how much it meant to both of them.

One of the reporters said, "Addie, what would you like to have most for Christmas?"

She was quiet for a moment and then looked at her mother and finally turned back to the reporter. "I'd like to have my Daddy home. I asked Santa Claus if he could bring Daddy home, but he said he wasn't sure he could do that."

***

By three o'clock Friday afternoon, Rose, Taylor, Juanita, her sister and two cousins were in the kitchen baking and sorting various cookies. There were chocolate chip cookies, sugar and gingerbread cookies and, of course, a cookie thief.

"Steven, how many cookies have you stolen?"

"Now, Rose, I just sampled one or two to make sure..."

"One or two! Steven, I saw you with at least four or five in your hands."

"Maybe it was a few more. But I wanted to be sure they were fit for human consumption."

"Out," she commanded, pointing to the door. "Out and stay out. Go help Jackson, Jose and George. I'm sure they could use your help carrying wood for the bonfire."

A few minutes later he met Jackson and saw that he, Jose and George had cleared a large space for the bonfire. Under Jackson's direction, they were already placing the kindling wood in the circle.

And, it was evident that he had some degree of expertise in correctly preparing for a large fire.

He looked over at Steve and smiled. "Use to do this often during my days in the military school."

"Well, I'm just gonna stand back and let you run the show."

Steve watched as the trio placed the seasoned logs around in the circle, all properly spaced to allow for enough oxygen to feed the flames.

At four o'clock, Taylor summoned them to the house for an early dinner of cold-cut subs, potato salad, potato chips and a teasing helping of the homemade cookies.

Jose became an instant hit with everyone when he managed to arrange a date with Juanita's sister in under two minutes of first meeting her.

He was honored for his "Romeo" maneuver with a lively round of applause and a pat on the back from George.

In George's case it took more than subtle prodding to get him to ask, Rosita, one of the two cousins for a date. Jose was beginning to think he might have to ask for him, but at last he mustered up the nerve and found he too had a date. However, there would be no "Red Hot Lover" or "Romeo" label bestowed upon him.

After dining, Jackson changed into his riding attire for the evening and he and Steve went to the barn to ready the wagon and horses.

While hitching the horses to the wagon Jackson said, "Mr. Whitefield, I noticed your wife always calls you Steven. Is there a particular reason?"

He chuckled. "From the day we first met, she's never called me anything but Steven. Even after all these years together, she still refuses to call me Steve. Says it just wouldn't feel right to call me Steve and please don't ask me why, I don't know."

They worked together much like a well-oiled machine and in no time had the horses hitched to the wagon and ready to go. A bale of straw was tossed into the back and spread evenly over the floor of the wagon. Then, Steve climbed aboard, Jackson opened the door and the wagon was rolling to its intended destination not far from the barn.

Jackson turned his full attention to preparing Christmas and Bronson for their roles. As he said, he would decorate the horses and set about winding Polo Wrap around their legs from hoof to knee joint. The right front legs were adorned in bright red, while the left front in dark green. The right rear legs were wrapped in dark green and left rear legs in bright red.

Next, he put on their reins and saddled them and added the final touch. Each had a set of bright red, imitation reindeer antlers placed on their heads just behind the top rein strap.

He patted Bronson on the neck. "As soon as your lovely mistress arrives, we'll be on our way."

Ten

The moment Taylor saw the horses she began smiling. "You weren't joking about decorating them. I love it. And, the antlers add an extra touch of Christmas spirit."

"Well, Your Highness, are you ready for the party?"

She laughed. "Let's go." She paused for a second. "By the way, Andrew, Beth, Josh and Anna can't make it. Josh has a bug and Anna's trying to catch it."

"Sorry to hear they can't make it."

As he gave her a leg up to help her mount Bronson, she saw the smile on his face. But a very different smile, a smile that said he was truly happy. Still, there was something else she hadn't seen in him before. He showed an air of excitement, much like you'd expect to see in someone much younger.

He led Christmas out of the barn and closed the door before mounting up. A second later he and Taylor were riding side by side and slowly making their way to the field on the house side of the driveway.

The bonfire was already burning brightly and the flames rose high in the crisp night air. The seasoned wood sizzled and popped, sending red-hot embers a few feet upward before they faded from a brilliant burnt orange, dimmed to black and fell back into the fire.

Two busloads of children and parents had already arrived and a third was on the way when Jackson and Taylor arrived.

Pete Wells pulled his wagon from the driveway into the field, turned and stopped, leaving about 15 feet between his and Steve's wagon. They looked at each other and laughed when they saw they'd chosen the same reins for their horses. The sleigh reins, with bells running the full length of the leather from horse to driver would add a rhythmic jingle to the ride.

With the arrival of the third bus, Diane Wilson and a number of volunteer parents began to calm the chaos and organize the kids and the remaining parents into groups. Naturally, everybody wanted to be in the two groups going first. So, it required greater effort to quiet the others who felt being third or more meant they'd have to wait forever before their turn.

Helen Davidson and a small group of military wives were on the third bus and thrilled to have been invited. While they stood and talked with other parents, Addie saw Jackson. She waved and called out to him and he quickly turned and rode to her.

He dismounted and she rushed to him. He quickly dropped to one knee and gladly accepted her hug and quick kiss on the cheek.

"Mr. Jackson, can I ride with you?" she gushed. "Please, can I ride with you?"

Her mother tried to intervene, but Jackson had already told her she could ride with him.

"Will that cause any problems?" Helen said.

"None at all, Ma'am. I'd be happy to have her with me."

"What's your horse's name?" Addie said.

"Her name is Christmas."

"Really!"

"Yes, that's her name."

"Wow! Mommy, I'm gonna ride a horse called Christmas!"

"I think that's a perfect horse to ride."

A moment later Jackson climbed back into the saddle and, with a little help from Helen Davidson lifted Addie up and into his arms. Soon she was seated behind him with her arms wrapped tightly around his waist.

He eased Christmas around and walked back to Taylor who was talking with Diane.

He smiled. "I believe I have a passenger for a little while."

Taylor nodded. "Well, she is certainly one very happy young lady."

Before he could answer, Diane said, "Well, you've broken my heart by not driving a wagon. Remember I was supposed to ride with you?"

"Sorry. Mr. Whitfield has seniority and he wanted to take up the driver's chores. I can't argue with the boss."

She stepped closer and put her hand up on his knee. "Well, I'd be willing to forgive you... on one condition."

"Oh? And what's that?"

"I could climb up there with you later this evening and we could enjoy a ride under the stars."

He smiled. "We might be able to arrange that."

She squeezed his knee. "I'm counting on it."

As he rode away with Addie, Taylor said, "Diane, I don't believe you did that."

"What? What did I do?"

"Do," she snapped. "You... You practically threw yourself at him."

"Oh, I did not. Besides..." She paused for a few seconds and stared at Taylor. "You... you're jealous."

"I'm not jealous. I..."

"Oh, my." Diane laughed. "Oh, Taylor, he got to you. Yes, I can see it in your yes. You've fallen for this guy."

"No. No," she snapped, hoping no one else could hear their conversation. "That's... that's ridiculous. I'd never... I mean..."

Diane smiled. "You can say whatever you want, but words can't hide what I see in your eyes."

"Let's just change the subject. I don't wanna waste any more time trying to convince you that I don't care for Jackson."

"Okay. If that's what you want." She looked Taylor straight in the eyes. "But you can lie to me and everyone else, but you can't lie to your heart."

With that Diane turned and walked away. But now she was more determined than ever to have that ride with Jackson. Though it wasn't to make Taylor jealous. She wanted to know if Jackson had feelings for Taylor.

It wasn't long before other children began clamoring for a ride with Jackson or Taylor. So, the special treat for the children was a quick ride on Christmas or Bronson and then back to wait their turn for the ride in the wagon.

Taylor was enjoying her part in making the kids happy, but she saw that Jackson was really having fun. He laughed and joked with the parents and gave the children from the military families a little extra attention without upsetting the others.

When the last wagon ride was completed, it was time for the hotdogs to be cooked over the open fire. The children were ecstatic when the adults let them take one of the sturdy sticks provided and roast their very own hotdog. Of course, when they heard they'd be toasting marshmallows later the shouts of glee echoed across the pastures and heightened the merriment.

As the evening wore on, it was expected that the children would begin to tire. But the excitement of everything happening around them seemed to push their energy level into overdrive.

Jackson and Taylor tethered Christmas and Bronson to a wagon and mingled with the crowd. It wasn't long before they were swallowed up in the sea of humanity and found themselves going in opposite directions.

Even in the crowd Diane was able to locate Jackson and pull

him aside. Suddenly, he found she was very persuasive. She had him by the arm and leading him to the wagons and horses.

He mounted up, removed his left foot from the stirrup and gave Diane a hand up. As soon as she was seated behind him she wrapped her arms tightly around him and snuggled as close as possible.

As he eased Christmas back from the wagon, Bronson gave a whinny. Jackson laughed. "I'll bring her back. I promise."

Diane saw that as a perfect opening. "Well, it looks like your horse and Taylor's have a thing for each other."

"Yeah, they do. I think it was love at first sight."

She hugged a little tighter. "Like you and Taylor."

"Wh... What?" he sputtered.

"Like you and Taylor. Love at first sight."

Diane caught him completely by surprise. "I... I don't know where you got that idea." He shook his head while trying to find an answer. "No, sir. We... we just don't get along that well. I mean, almost not at all."

"Really? So, the sparks that I see flying around the two of you don't mean anything."

He shook his head again. "Sparks? I don't know what you're talkin' about. We kinda tolerate each other, but that's about it."

"So, that means you're still available?"

"Available?"

She smiled. "You know, I could ask you for a date and it wouldn't be a problem."

"Well... Well, I... I have a lot to do around here. I'm... I'm busy almost all the time."

"So, there's no time for love in your life. Is that it?"

He reined Christmas to a stop. "Uh... Well, I guess we'd better get back to the others."

She laughed. "I think you're right."

When she dismounted, he located Taylor and told her he'd

take the horses back to the barn. He didn't wait for her to answer, but turned and hurried away.

He walked Christmas and Bronson to the barn, removed their decorative wrappings and antlers, saddles and bridles. He gave them a quick brushing with a promise that he'd return later.

Around the bonfire some of the parents joined together and began singing Christmas Carols. Soon more added their voices to the impromptu concert and there was little doubt that the Christmas Season was in full bloom in Cedar Falls.

In the midst of their singing, and seemingly from nowhere, Santa Claus appeared. Now, the children's level of elation soared far beyond anything their parents could have imagined.

Cries of, "Santa, Santa," filled the air as he began walking among them and handing out small boxes of Christmas cookies and candy canes. Even the adults were treated to a box of cookies and a Merry Christmas from Santa.

Eventually he made his way around through the crowd and moved by the wagons to approach Taylor. He stood close behind her and just to her right before touching her gently on the shoulder and handing her a box of cookies and a candy cane.

He stepped quickly back to his left and softly said, "Young lady, I certainly hope you've been nice."

She spun quickly and reached, but he magically disappeared into the crowd again before she could catch him by the arm. She scanned the mass of children and adults, but it seemed the crafty Old Elf had mystically vanished. She lowered her head and smiled.

In time the energy level of the children began subsiding and the parents breathed a sigh of relief. One by one and in small groups they began thanking Steve and Rose Whitfield for their hospitality and a truly wonderful evening of Christmas fun.

Steve spent extra time talking with Helen and Addie and made sure he had Wyatt's full name, rank, unit and address. When asked why, he said he'd like to send an appropriate Christmas gift to him and his unit.

The last bus pulled away, with a much quieter crowd aboard, and headed back to Cedar Falls Elementary School. But there would surely be some fond memoires and dreams about their evening at the Whitfield farm.

When Jose and George began extinguishing the last remnants of the bonfire, Taylor slipped away and went to the barn.

Bronson was in his stall and Jackson was brushing Christmas when she walked in. She quietly strolled down the aisle toward him and watched the way he gently brushed her.

"Party finally over?" he said, glancing at her.

"Yes. The children finally ran out of energy and I think some of the parents were just as tired."

He smiled. "Well, I'm sure it was worth it."

"You really enjoyed yourself too," she said, watching him as he continued slowly brushing Christmas.

He nodded. "Yes, I did."

"You know, it looked to me as if you were as excited as the kids. You were having as much or more fun than they were."

He shrugged. "Well, I couldn't show up and be a grumpy old Grinch and ruin the night for everybody."

She moved closer to him. "I think there was something else going on. Tonight was what you didn't have growing up and you were trying to chase away those memories from long ago."

He turned, put the bush down and picked up another and went on brushing Christmas.

"So, I'm right. This is what you didn't have growing up."

He looked over at her. "Why is my life so important to you? Why should what I had or didn't have when I was growing up mean anything to you."

"You just don't wanna open that door, do you?"

"And you call me impossible," he said, shaking his head.

"Okay. Let's change the topic. Why'd you do it?"

"Hey, she was the one buggin' me about the ride. I just did it to get her off my back."

"Oh, I wasn't talking about Diane."

"Then I don't know what you're talkin' about."

She stepped directly in front of him. "Now, you're gonna try and tell me that wasn't you in the Santa Claus outfit?"

"Santa Claus outfit?"

"Oh, no you don't, Jackson Riley. You're not gonna stand there and pretend that wasn't you. I knew it was you playing Santa when you made that comment about me being nice."

"Okay. Okay, it was me."

She smiled, threw her hands in the air and said, "At last, a confession from the heart. Yes, it was you and you did it as much for yourself as you did for those kids. You wanted desperately to make them happy and in the end, you were as happy as they were... maybe happier. Admit it."

He took a deep breath and said, "I did enjoy it. And I did it to make them happy. But when I saw their reactions and how excited they were, I just got lost in the moment. I guess I didn't expect to see them react that way. I mean their level of happiness was far more than I anticipated."

She smiled again. "You opened the door a little. And I'm gonna keep on trying until you open it completely."

"Why is it..."

At that very moment, Christmas put her nose in the middle of Taylor's back and nudged her right into Jackson's arms.

Suddenly, they were mere inches from touching lips, looking into each other's eyes and frozen in place.

The silence dragged on until Taylor said, "Your... your horse pushed me."

"She... she did?"

"Yes."

He continued looking into her eyes. "I... I, uh... I guess I should reprimand her."

"You should."

"When?"

"Now would be a good time."

"Oh, yeah." He moved his head slightly to the right to glance over Taylor's left shoulder and said, "Bad horse."

"You... you didn't sound very convincing."

"I... I didn't?"

My heart's pounding so hard, I swear I can hear it. She took a quick breath. "No, you didn't."

"Well, I... I didn't wanna yell in your ear."

"You would never yell at your horse." *I've gotta get out of here,* she thought. *But what am I gonna do?* Suddenly, she went on the offensive. "I bet you trained her to do that."

"What? You mean trained her to push you?"

She tried her best to glare at him. "You did, didn't you?"

They were still only inches apart and neither showed any sign of wanting to back away. He shook his head and said, "Why would I do that?"

"**Ha**. And you know why. You just wanted to put your arms around me."

"What?" he blurted. "You need to get over yourself. I'd rather put my arms around a cluster of poison ivy."

"Yeah. Well, you're still holding on to me."

"Hey, you grabbed me first," he snapped.

"You grabbed back."

"And, I suppose it's all Christmas's fault?"

"I think I'd better leave," she said, lowering her eyes.

"Oh, that's the best idea you've had all night."

"Let go of me," she said, trying to raise her voice.

Still looking into her eyes, he began smiling. "Do you wanna have a three count so we can let go at the same time?"

She suddenly pushed back, stammering, "Oh, you... you...

you're so… so… so aggravating." With that she turned and hurried toward the door and disappearing into the night.

When the door closed behind her he looked at Christmas. "I almost blew it. Man, that was close. Do you know how close I came to kissing her?"

Christmas looked at him and shook her head up and down three times.

"You know, I'm really beginning to wonder just how smart you are. In fact, I'm wondering if you knew what you were doing all along." He reached out and gently rubbed her nose. "Did you push Taylor into my arms on purpose?"

She turned her head slightly to the left and he saw a gleam in her eye.

"Christmas, I swear you're smiling."

She licked him on the back of his hand, went into her stall and closed the gate.

Eleven

Taylor sat at her night table staring at her reflection in the mirror. *How can one man cause so much confusion in my life? I thought I had my life planned to the letter of perfection. Then, out of nowhere, Jackson Riley doesn't slowly appear, he slams into my life like a... a hurricane. He tosses me in a water trough, he compares me to a horse's backside and in a round about way tells me I'm a self-centered brat.*

I'm working on every imaginable way to hate him and then he makes me laugh. He does it with his devilish smile or some off the cuff remark and I can't help it. I just laugh and forget all about hating him.

Naturally, I try all over again to hate him and then I see the way he treats his horse. He really loves her. And, it's the same with all the other animals, he's so good to them. They have no fear of him and they know they'll get their tummy rubs and back scratches and he'll pretend they're bothering him. But there he is a minute later giving treats to all of them.

Oh, but that's not all. He has to drop a real bomb on me at the mall with Addie Davidson. He just couldn't turn around and walk away from her. No, sir, not Jackson Riley. Mr. big, strong and powerful has to wrap his arms around her and give her the hug she wants and make every one of us break down and cry. So, Mr. hard and tough Marine has a soft spot in his heart for kids and animals, and it's getting to me.

Then, there's tonight. I'm still shaking from that moment of almost complete surrender. I can't believe we were that close and didn't kiss. What happened? Why didn't we? My heart's starting to pound again just thinking about it. And, I think my heart's pounding right now because I do care for him. I care far more than I want to admit and it scares me. Maybe I'm afraid because I don't know how he feels about me. Sometimes, I believe he really has feelings for me and then, all of a sudden there's the cloud of uncertainty again.

At last she slid under the covers and tried her very best to push away love's confusing questions and hope for a restful sleep.

***

Jackson walked into the barn earlier then usual, but was nonetheless greeted with a chorus of demanding whinnies, not to mention the dog yaps and cat meows.

"Okay, boys and girls, settle down. I'll feed you as soon as possible." He smiled, knowing he was going to hear their demands to be fed regardless of the time he arrived.

He began with Comet and Cupid and worked his way from stall to stall, pouring grain into buckets and listening to the munches of contentment.

Christmas was the last to be fed, but first he had to give her a good morning kiss and then pour the gain into her bucket. She'd come to expect the kiss before eating and quickly accepted it as part of her daily ritual.

She had also grown accustomed to being the last horse taken to pasture. But that also meant there was special time together with Jackson and being brushed and slipped a few treats before going out to join the others.

Now, it was simply a matter of waiting while Jackson fed the dogs and cats, after their daily tummy rubs and back scratches.

He opened her stall gate and she slowly walked out and stood in her usual spot while he selected something from the grooming kit to begin her grooming. Today it was the hoof pick.

"Okay, sweetheart, time to check the tire pressure," he said as he dropped to one knee. He tapped her left front hoof and she raised it for inspection. "Not bad at all. Just a little dirt, but I can brush that out."

With the hooves cleaned it was time to comb the mane and tail. He began with her tail and the comb glided easily through the dark coarse hair. Of course, with the daily care she received it was almost impossible to find a tangle in her tail or mane.

Next came the brushing and he began brushing her lightly under the chin, working back to her neck and down the front of her chest.

"Well, Christmas, I still have some things I've gotta get off my plate. Look, I'm gonna confess to you that I have some really strong feelings for Taylor. And, I know I need to open that door to let her in. But I just don't think the time's right… at least not yet.

"I've gotta do my very best to find my mom and try to make things right between us. If I can find her and get our relationship on the right track, it'll sure make things a lot easier for me to tell Taylor how I feel. I don't wanna rush in like a fool and end up hurting her. She doesn't deserve that."

He paused and gave her an apple treat and went on. "I know there's a lot I should tell her and there's sure a lotta things I wouldn't tell her. Those things are just too ugly and she doesn't need to hear about them and sometimes I wonder if I should really tell you.

"Between you and me, I sure would like to get all of this outta the way before Christmas.

"Okay, I'd better get you out to the pasture. I've gotta get busy in here and clean the stalls."

He walked her out to the pasture, but when he returned, he found Taylor waiting.

"Dad called Jose and George and asked them to come in this morning and take care of the stalls. He wants to talk with you about something over breakfast."

"Okay," he said, while reaching for a treat for Rooster and Rita. "Are you havin' breakfast with us?"

"Yes, he invited me too."

"Good. I'll go grab a quick shower and change."

As they walked out of the barn she said, "About last night, I think I owe you an apology?"

"Apology? For what?"

"For the way I acted."

He smiled. "Taylor you have nothing to apologize for."

"But…"

He reached out and gently touched a finger to her lips. "No apology, please. Nothing happened that requires a bended knee 'I'm sorry'."

"Then we agree that everything's fine between us."

"Absolutely," he said, his smile growing. "Everything's as good between us now as it was the day we met."

She shook her head. "I should've known you'd find a way to make this easy."

"So, for one reason or another, we're gonna call a truce."

"Agreed."

He nodded. "Shall we seal the truce with a handshake?"

She laughed. "Okay, but no tricks with the handshake."

After a quick handshake they were off to the house and a shower and change of clothes for Jackson.

***

When the trio arrived at the Cedar Falls Diner, Barb wasted no time in pouncing on opportunity. "Ah, the lovebirds back again. What are you battling over this time?"

Jackson pointed to Taylor. "She accused me of training my horse to perform devious tricks."

"If your horse takes after you, you wouldn't need to train it," Barb said, as she picked up menus and led them to a table.

Taylor laughed. "I agree with you, Barb."

"Hey, I thought we agreed to a truce," Jackson said, looking over at Taylor.

Barb looked from one to the other. "Well, I do hope you sealed that truce with a kiss."

Taylor snapped off a quick retort, beating Jackson to the punch. "Oh, yes. I let him kiss my horse."

Barb shook her head. "Poor horse."

"Merry Christmas to you too, Barb," he shot back. "I know what list Santa has you on and it's not the nice side."

Steve Whitfield picked up his menu and muttered, "One of these days I've gotta find out what's goin' on here."

Jackson decided to try and get ahead of Barb. "The usual for me. One dumpster and a coffee."

She nodded. "Will that be a dumpster with or without?"

"With or without what?"

"Flies."

He took a deep breath. "Without. Winter flies just aren't as crunchy as spring and summer."

"Hummm. I'll hafta remember that." She turned to Taylor and said, "And you, Miss, what will you have?"

After their orders were taken, Steve took off his glasses and said, "I've put a call in to Senator Blake and I'm gonna ask him to see if he can work on gettin' Gunnery Sergeant Davidson home for Christmas."

Jackson nodded. "That would be fantastic and it sure would make Addie and her mom happy. But, does Senator Blake have that much pull?"

"John and I go way back and I know he has a lotta friends...

very high-ranking friends in the military, and especially the Marine Corps."

"It would be great if you could pull it off, but there isn't a lotta time and it could prove very difficult."

"I know," Steve said, reaching for his coffee. "But John has a great deal of influence among his fellow senators as well as those in the military. If anybody can do it, he can."

"What can I do to help?"

After taking a sip of coffee Steve said, "What I really need is your advice."

"Yes, Sir. Whatever you want?"

"I see a lotta these *surprise* reunions on TV with dozens or hundreds of people around. What's your opinion on that?"

Jackson was quiet for a few seconds. "Well, sir, if it was me and my homecoming with my family, I'd rather keep it private. Just between me and my family and maybe some very close friends."

"Okay."

Jackson went on. "I think that would be something I'd only wanna share with my family. It's gotta be a very emotional reunion and it should belong only to them. There'll be time later on to greet other friends and neighbors."

"I agree with you a hundred percent. And, I figured that's what you'd say, but I wanted your input."

"Thank you for asking," Jackson said, reaching for his coffee cup.

"If I can get this approved, I might need your help with the arrangements."

"Yes, Sir. You can count on me."

Steve nodded. "Anyway, I was thinking of tryin' to arrange something at a hotel near one of the airports. You know, get one of their smaller banquet rooms and set up a breakfast or lunch for the family members."

"I like that. It keeps the press outta the picture."

"Yeah. I don't want the media anywhere near their reunion."

He smiled. "Do you have a plan for gettin' Gunny Davidson from the airport to the hotel."

"That's where you come in. I was thinkin' about havin' a limo pick him up at the airport and take him to the hotel. But, since you've had a face to face with him and can recognize him, I thought you could meet him. I'll leave it up to you whether or not you wanna accompany him to the hotel."

"Let me think about that. I don't wanna take anything at all away from the family reunion." He took a sip of his coffee. "I guess I could follow the limo to the hotel, make sure he's escorted to the room and disappear."

Steve nodded. "Now we just hafta hope and pray that Blake can work some Christmas magic and get him home."

Breakfast was served and after eating, Steve said he had to meet with some associates regarding a business venture and excused himself.

Jackson and Taylor walked to the truck and she noticed that he seemed lost in thought.

"Is everything okay?"

"Do you think we could stop by a church before we go back to the farm?"

She was surprised by his question, but after a few seconds said, "Yes. If that's what you want."

He looked out the window and then at Taylor. "Uh… This might sound strange, but you pick the church."

"Well, we attend St. Martin's Catholic Church, if that's okay with you."

He nodded. "Uh… Sure. That'll do just fine. Just point the way."

About ten minutes later he and Taylor walked into the church and, after a few steps, he stopped and looked around. He very slowly scanned the interior of the church, beginning at the back and shifting to the front. He took a few steps toward the front of the church and stopped. Once again, he looked all around, this time turning and glancing up to the choir loft.

"You seem… I don't know how to say it, but…"

He forced a smile. "Confused or surprised?

"I'm not sure. It's almost like… like this is your first time in a church."

He shook his head. "It's just seems like it's been a very long time since I've been in a church." He looked from the back to the front again. "I missed this when I was a kid. Church was absolutely off limits. I know my mom wanted to go and take me, but my father wouldn't allow it."

"I… I'm sorry."

"Hey, it's not your fault." He glanced at the altar. "I'm sure there was a time when my mom took me to church, but I was much too young to understand what was going on. In fact, I don't know if the church was Catholic or something else."

"Did you go to church services when you were in school or the Marine Corps?" she said, watching him closely as he continued to look around at the church.

"I did," he said, with a nod. "But it always felt like there was something missing. And, I just can't tell you what it was."

"There's a Mass here this evening at five. Would you like to go?"

"Uh… Sure."

"I… I could go with you if you want me to."

He smiled. "I'd like that. And maybe we could go to dinner after church… if you don't have a date."

She looked into his eyes and said, "I do now."

He nodded. "Yes, you do."

Oh, Taylor, she thought. *What just happened? Is this really going to be a date, or will it be just like everything else between us?*

***

They returned to the farm and Jackson brought Christmas out of the pasture and into the indoor arena. He put on her reins and took a few slow laps around the paddock before working on her training by touch again.

She performed like a champion, never missing a beat as she backed up, turned right and left with just a touch of his hand. He smiled and said, "Good girl. You are one smart lady."

As if the words of praise were her cue, Christmas began to prance and took a full lap around the arena. Had there been an audience she would have probably been given a standing ovation.

Jackson laughed. "You know, Mr. Whitfield probably hit the nail on the head. You outsmarted Swanson just to get away from him and his nasty treatment. Well, I'll never treat you the way he did."

He slid off her back and she followed him into the barn and stopped in front of her stall.

A moment later Rooster and Rita appeared and hurried to see Christmas. She lowered her head and both gave her an abundance of "kisses" and in return she gave each a very gentle nudge.

Next, they rushed to Jackson, sat in front of him and began vigorously wagging their tails. Of course, this could only mean one thing—they wanted a treat.

"I guess you want a cookie."

They answered with a sharp yap and continued wagging their tails, watching in anticipation as he reached into his pocket. Then, Jackson the magician pulled two biscuits from his pocket and held them up for them to see.

Suddenly, they were jumping in the air and spinning around in circles, first to the right and then left. They paused, gave a quick yap and spun around again.

"Okay, kids. That's enough showin' off," he said and tossed a biscuit to each.

As the dogs began munching their biscuits, he moved toward Christmas to groom her. But her quick glance over his right shoulder clearly said, "Look behind you."

He turned and saw Hank, Sylvester and Sylvia sitting side-by-side and looking at him. Actually, it was more of a "how dare you glare." Indeed, they were letting him know that he'd violated protocol by not providing them with a treat as well.

He laughed. "Okay. Okay, I'm sorry. I didn't know you were there."

In a matter of seconds, it was cat treats all around and they seemed happy. Whether or not they'd forgive him for his mistake any time soon was another matter.

He walked to Christmas and immediately gave her an apple treat. "Hey, I'm not gonna get on your bad side. Here have another one."

He gave her a quick kiss on the nose and began brushing her. He brushed her coat for about 45 minutes before returning her to the pasture.

He returned to the barn and began setting up for the evening feeding. He emptied and refilled the water buckets in each stall and then filled the grain buckets. Next, came the hay for everybody and he was well ahead of schedule.

For the next two hours he worked on his computer attempting to locate his mother. He found two prospects that offered some hope and he dug deeper into their backgrounds. One seemed to stand out above the other and he hurried to dig deeper into her past only to have his hopes frustrated once again.

He looked at the clock on the wall, stood up and headed to the barn. He would bring the horses in earlier today, which would give him ample time to shower and dress for church.

He felt a little flutter of nervous anticipation as he dressed. He hadn't been to church in at least three months, but today he was looking forward to the opportunity. And, suddenly, he realized he wouldn't be walking into church alone.

Twelve

Jackson walked into St. Martin's Church with Taylor and was immediately recognized by one of the ushers, who walked over to him and shook his hand. He thanked Jackson for his service and what he'd done for Addie Davidson.

A moment later he was following Taylor to a pew and taking her lead, genuflecting and then kneeling. Indeed, this wasn't a total mystery to him and he offered a prayer of thanks for his blessings, which included the Whitfield family and his horse.

Initially, the church had been relatively empty, but was now filling quickly. There were more than a few curious glances cast in the direction of Jackson and Taylor. Were people surprised to see Taylor with a man who was a relative stranger? Or, perhaps they had watched the television clip of Jackson and Addie and were surprised to see him in person.

There were a few parents who had attended the wagon ride and hotdog roast at the Whitfield Farm the night before, who saw them and waved. Of course, there were a few children who also recognized them and their waves were a bit more enthusiastic than those of their parents.

Jackson and Taylor smiled and acknowledge their waves and

hoped the children would settle down and remain calm during the service.

At five o'clock sharp Father Kurt entered the church from the back. The organist began playing *O Come, O Come Emanuel* and soon the Altar Boys, followed by Father Kurt began walking down the aisle toward the front of the church.

As the Mass began Jackson easily recognized the service and knew he'd attended more than a few Catholic Masses. Still, there was so much more he needed to discover before he could be certain where he belonged. Although there was one thing he was sure of, he felt comfortable with Taylor beside him.

At the conclusion of the service they held back and allowed the majority of the congregation to exit. Then they walked slowly out and were greeted by Father Kurt.

"It's a pleasure to meet you and shake your hand," Father Kurt said to Jackson.

"Thank you, Sir... I mean, Father."

He smiled. "That was a wonderful thing you did for Addie Davidson and her mother."

"Father, I did it for a brother. He would've done the same for me."

"This might be true, but you also did it for a little girl who missed her father. You brightened her day and I believe you gave her a ray of hope."

He took a deep breath. "Father, there are times when all of us need a ray of hope."

Father Kurt nodded. "Maybe more so now than ever."

They talked for a few more minutes and Jackson and Taylor said goodnight and walked to the truck.

He started the engine and said, "Okay, what's it gonna be, Italian, Chinese, Japanese, Mexican, or a good old fashion Texas size steak?"

She laughed. "I didn't realize you were gonna make it so

difficult to choose. Right now, everything sounds so delicious. But, I'm sure you're a down home meat and potatoes man. So, let's go to Emerson's Steak House."

"Okay. And, it doesn't sound like it's a chain restaurant."

She smiled. "Oh, believe me, it's not." She was quiet for few seconds and then laughed. "They probably have a few dishes on the menu that might even fill you up."

"Uh... No dumpsters I hope."

"No dumpsters."

It wasn't long before they were seated in a very cozy corner of the dining room. The lights throughout were dimmed just enough to add a relaxing and intimate atmosphere. Each table had a lighted candle, with the larger tables having at least two. The chairs at the tables were covered in rustic dark brown leather, which hinted of the Old West and they were indeed very comfortable.

The remainder of Emerson's décor offered every Cowboy at heart and lovers of western lore a place to feel as if they were dining on the range. The walls throughout held paintings of cowboys riding their trusty steeds, herds of wild horses, Indians riding their ponies beside a large herd of Bison, a pack of wolves howling on a snow-covered mountaintop and Elk and Black Tailed Deer grazing on the grass.

The waiters and waitresses wore casual western attire of blue jeans, western shirts and cowboy boots, but the maître D' was more formal. He dressed in a black tuxedo, with a short waist jacket, a ruffled white shirt, black string tie and cowboy boots.

Taylor ordered a glass of red wine and Jackson asked for a Johnnie Walker Black Label on the rocks. Taylor's dinner order was a petit filet with a large garden salad in lieu of the standard starches and vegetables. Jackson, of course, went for the gusto ordering the King Cut Prime Rib, rare with baked potato and mushrooms.

Taylor smiled. "Would you prefer they just deliver a whole steer to the table so you can cut off a side or hind quarter?"

"If the prime rib doesn't do the trick, I might do that."

"I'm betting that you'll eat every last morsel and still have room for dessert."

He laughed. "A good meal should be topped off with a very appropriate dessert."

"If I ate the way you do, I'd weigh 400 pounds."

"Whoa! Don't even go there. I can't imagine you being anything but fit and trim."

"I'll do my best to stay sleek and trim and keep you happy."

"Oh. You'll do that to keep me happy?"

The arrival of dinner rescued her from having to respond to his last remark and for that she was grateful.

Taylor finished her meal and smiled as she watched him eat until his plate looked as if it just came out of the dishwasher. She took a sip of wine and said, "You know, it's fun watching you eat."

"A new hobby?"

"No. I mean it's like you don't just sit at a table and eat what's on your plate, but actually enjoy your meal."

He nodded. "Well, I do enjoy a good meal. And, there were times when I didn't have the opportunity to sit back and truly savor a well-prepared meal. So, I learned to appreciate good food when it was served."

"I guess you ate a lotta meals on the run when you were a Marine."

"Yeah, and MREs don't offer prime rib."

At that moment the waitress arrived and asked if they would care to have dessert.

Taylor declined, but Jackson said, "That warm brownie with ice cream and hot chocolate sauce looks like a great way to top off a fantastically delicious meal."

The waitress smiled. "You won't be disappointed."

"I'm sure I won't."

When the waitress left, Taylor said, "You seem to have a

very special relationship with your horse."

He smiled. "She's a sweetheart. I'm so happy that I came along when I did. She didn't deserve to be mistreated and she sure didn't need to be sold at auction."

"You're her knight in shining armor."

"I like to think of it as being her best friend."

She nodded. "And I guess it's safe to say she's your best friend."

"Absolutely. I talk to her all the time and tell her my secrets and problems."

She seemed puzzled. "You tell Christmas your secrets and your problems?"

"Sure. Don't you talk to Bronson and tell him your problems and secrets?"

"No. I mean I don't share secrets or anything like that."

He gave a shrug. "You should."

"Why? I mean, I never thought about it before."

"Well, I'd always heard that a horse was the best therapist in the world. You spend so much time with them and, even if you don't realize it, when you leave the barn after grooming him or her, you feel better. You feel relaxed."

She sat back in her chair and stared at him. "You're right. I do feel better after spending time with Bronson, riding and grooming him. I do talk to him, but not in the way you talk to Christmas."

"You should try it. The best part is, they listen to all your problems and even your most intimate secrets and they never tell anyone."

She shook her head. "I never thought of it that way. They can listen to everything you say, but never repeat it. And when you think about it, how many human friends will actually keep your intimate secrets to themselves?"

"Not that many. Maybe none. They listen to your secret and before you know it, they wanna make it their secret and share it with somebody else. Then boom! Your secret's out there being shared with the world."

Taylor suddenly felt bold. "Have you told Christmas any secrets about me?"

He nodded and looked directly into her eyes. "Yes, I have."

Her heart was off and running along with a mass of hopeful thoughts. *I shouldn't have asked that question. But I wanted to know. More than that, I wanna know what those secrets are. I hope he told her he cares for me. I hope he told her he… I… I hope he told her he loves me. Oh, no. Am I crazy for wanting that?*

Once again, the waitress saved the day when she arrived and placed his desert on the table.

"Wow!" Taylor said. "That's enough for five people."

The waitress gave her a spoon. "Well, I thought he'd be kind enough to share with you."

They were quiet as they ate dessert, but Taylor's appetite was no match for Jackson's. She again smiled as she watched him take the last spoonful.

He gave a nod of satisfaction. "Well, that certainly was the perfect ending for a perfect dinner."

He signaled to the waitress and asked for the check.

"That's okay, sir. Your meal's been taken care of."

"It's been paid for?"

"Yes, Sir."

"Who…"

"Sir, I'm sorry but they asked to remain anonymous."

"Miss, this was not a dollar ninety-eight dinner. This had to cost over a hundred dollars."

She nodded. "Sir, regardless of the cost, your meal has been paid for."

He shook his head. "Well, I can at least give you a tip for your outstanding service."

"Sir, that's been taken care of as well and he was more than a little generous."

"Please offer him my sincere thanks." He paused and added, "And you can tell him if I ever learn his identify, the next time it's my treat."

She smiled. "Yes, Sir. I'll pass that along."

When they began the drive home Taylor said, "When should we get the Christmas tree?"

"I was thinkin' about that myself. How about Wednesday after I finish feeding and turning out the horses?"

"Okay, that sounds fine. Now, do you think we should go to a roadside stand or should we cut our own?"

"Let's cut our own," he said with a big smile. "I think that would make the tree more special."

"I agree. And there's a tree farm that's only about a half-hour drive from the house."

"Perfect. Then it's a date."

"Wow!" she said. "Two dates in less then a week. What will people think?"

"They might think we've lost our minds or... or..."

"Or what?"

"Uh... Or that we're best friends."

"That's what I thought too." Somehow, even though she was disappointed, she smiled. Suddenly, she decided to make the boldest move she'd even made in her entire life. "Jackson, you do know that sometimes best friends fall in love and get married."

"What!" he blurted as he turned his head quickly to the right to look at her and nearly ran off the road.

"Oh, nothing."

He regained control of the truck and thought *did she say what I thought she said, or was I hearing things?*

She kept the lead by saying, "So, after we put the tree up you and I can decorate it."

"You want me to help you decorate the tree?"

"Sure. We can do that Wednesday evening after dinner."

"Yeah. Okay, that sounds like fun."

"It can be lots of fun."

He glanced over at her. "You know, I've never decorated a Christmas tree before." He nodded. "I'm really lookin' forward to this."

She looked over at him and saw the smile on his face. He had a big grin on his face and she believed that he was really happy at the moment. And for the first time she realized that so often in the days since they met, she saw a hidden sadness in his eyes. It was there even when he smiled and she couldn't help but wonder why. What was it in his past that still haunted him?

She tried to push the thought aside, but it was no use. Then she wondered what it was like growing up in a home where there was no Christmas tree. What was it like never being allowed to attend church services?

His voice broke the silence. "Okay, ma'am, you've been delivered safely to your home by your friendly taxi service."

She laughed. "Too bad you didn't turn the meter on."

He opened the door for her and allowed her to get a few steps ahead. He leaned down, scooped up a handful of snow and cupped his bare hands together molding the fluffy power into a rather nice snowball.

Just as she reached the top step, he launched the snowball. It sailed high as he'd intended and struck the wood just above the porch. The snowball shattered into hundreds of tiny fragments that showered down over Taylor.

"That's cold," she screamed as she jumped on to the porch. She danced around while trying to brush the snow from the back of her neck and hair. She squealed, "That's so cold and it's running down my back."

He stepped up on to the porch and she took a half-hearted swing at him. He quickly caught her by the wrist and pulled. In an instant there they were again, mere inches apart.

Suddenly he was thinking *don't do it, Jackson. Don't do it. Don't you dare do it.*

Taylor on the other hand was thinking *Oh, God, why don't you just kiss me? You're really driving me crazy.*

He stepped back and said, "Okay. Time for you to get in the house before you violate curfew."

Before she knew it, he had opened the door and, with a hand on her back, was guiding her inside.

"Taylor, is everything okay?" said her mother who was seated on the sofa in the living room. "I heard you scream."

"Jackson hit me with a snowball."

"I did not hit you with a snowball. I hit the house with the snowball. You just happened to be standing in the wrong place and the snowball broke apart and fell on you.

She pointed a finger at him. "But you did it on purpose. You knew it was gonna fall apart and go down my back."

"Now wait a minute. I didn't know it would go down your back. That was just an added bonus."

"Bonus!" she yelled. "Bonus. I'll get you for this."

He smiled. "Well, if you'll excuse me, I've gotta go kiss my horse goodnight." He turned to walk away, but stopped and turned back. "I guess I'd better kiss you goodnight first."

She sucked in her breath and felt her heart racing. He reached out, took her by the hand and softly kissed the back of it. "Thank you for the pleasure of your company this evening." An instant later he was out the door and on the way to the barn.

"Jackson, Riley, you frustrate me. You aggravate me. You drive me crazy," she gushed. "You... you..."

"Taylor, would you like to sit down and talk?" her mother said, looking at her daughter and smiling.

"Yes. Yes, I would," she said, taking off her coat.

As she sat down in a chair across from the sofa, her mother

said, "Why don't we start with you telling me what's going on with you and Jackson?"

"Mom, he frustrates me. He drives me crazy."

"Really?"

"Yes. He... He's turned my whole world upside down." She shook her head. "I thought I had a perfect map for my future and he comes along and ruins everything."

"Why do you think that happened?"

"I should hate him. I wanted to hate him." She paused and took a deep breath. "And, the more I tried to hate him, the more I enjoyed being with him. I start to get angry and he makes me laugh. He compares me to a horse's backside and later on he's making a joke about it to a waitress and I'm finding it funny. I turn the table on him and we both enjoy it."

"So, you enjoy his company and the joking around, but I'm sure there're other things."

She nodded. "He's so good with children. He seems to really enjoy doing things for them, things that make them happy. And, the little girl at the mall, Addie Davidson... God, he made me cry when I saw him hug her." She shook her head. "I've never seen anyone treat animals the way he does. He talks with them and plays with them and I can see he's having so much fun. And, his horse... I can't believe how they just seem to belong together, like they were meant for each other. It's so easy to see she loves him."

Her mother smiled. "Now, I understand why you've fallen in love with him."

"Mom, that's insane. I'm... I'm..."

"Taylor, do you know how much you've changed since he walked into your life?"

"Changed?"

"Oh, yes. You began changing the day you first met him."

"I haven't..."

"Taylor, be honest with me. Be honest with yourself. Do

you know how many dates you've turned down since you came home?"

"Uh... Not really."

"At least seven that I'm aware of. A few months ago, you would've jumped at the opportunity to go out with some of those young men who called." She smiled. "At one time all of them would've been a candidate for that Mr. Right you were always so determined to find."

Taylor looked down for a second. "Then along comes Mr. Jackson Riley, who isn't a single thing I dreamed of as the man I wanted to spend my life with. Yet every minute I'm around him, the more I want to be with him."

"So, you admit you're in love with him."

"Mom, the day we first met he threw me in a horse trough. I bet dad didn't throw you in a horse trough."

"Well, no, your father didn't throw me in a horse trough."

"Mom... Mom, your tone of voice said something happened. What was it?"

"Taylor, your father locked me in a closet."

"What! He locked you in a closet!"

"Yes. I'd known your father for quite some time and he'd asked me out dozens of times and I always said no. He wasn't my Mr. Right. But, like Jackson with you, he made me laugh and he also told me I was nothing more than a spoiled brat."

"Dad, called you a spoiled brat?"

"And, he was right. Well, we were at a party... a very big party. He asked me to dance and I told him I wouldn't dance with him if the was the last man on earth.

"So, he said I needed a lesson in manners. The next thing I knew he had me by the arm, dragging me into the hallway. Then he opened the closet door, stuffed me in, closed and locked the door. I started pounding on the door, screaming at him to let me out. Of course, this drew a crowd and everybody thought it was the funniest thing ever."

"What happened next?"

"I guess it was about a half-hour later, he unlocked the door and let me out. He smiled and said, 'Have a nice day' and walked off. I was fuming. I screamed and yelled how much I hated him and added a few spicy expletives to make my point.

"Well, after I cooled off, I went looking for him. I searched for almost an hour before I saw him sitting alone on top of an old stone-wall. I walked toward him and as I got close, I could see this smile on his face. I decided that was it. I wasn't going to give him a chance to say a word. I stopped in front him, threw my arms around him and kissed him."

"Are you serious?"

"Absolutely," she said, her eyes gleaming. "I finally stepped back and said, 'Steven Whitfield, I've been in love with you forever and I'm gonna marry you'."

"What did he say?"

"He just smiled and said, 'When'?"

"Maybe I should do the same with Jackson."

"Not yet, Taylor. The time's not right."

"Why?"

"Call it a mother's intuition, but I'm certain Jackson's in love with you. I know there's something bothering him, I can feel it and see it in his eyes. Whatever it is, he needs to be free of it."

"Mom, you're right. I can see it too. I see sadness in his eyes sometimes, even if he smiles or laughs. I think a lot from his past bothers him. He's told me a little about his childhood and I know it wasn't pretty. But there's a lot more he hasn't told me."

"Take your time and be patient. Let Jackson work out his problem and don't push to find out what it is. If he wants to talk with you about it, he will on his terms."

"Okay. I'll let him open the door."

"That's the best thing you can do."

"By the way, how did you know I was in love with him?"

She smiled. "When he made that comment about kissing you goodnight, I thought you were about to faint."

She laughed. "It was that obvious?"

"Yes. And, I'll pray that you get what you want."

Thirteen

Jackson opened the stall gate and Christmas walked out just as he pulled an apple treat from his pocket. Soon she was munching on the tasty morsel and enjoying his soft scratching under her chin. Of course, there was the familiar nose kiss before he picked up a brush and began stroking her coat.

"You know, girl, it's really gettin' tough to keep my feelings under control around Taylor. Tonight almost did me in. I was so close to kissing her and, to be honest, I don't know why I didn't just take her in my arms, kiss her and tell her how I feel."

He gave her another treat and kept brushing. "I enjoyed my dinner with Taylor this evening and we talked about different things. But there are things I wouldn't tell her. In fact, I guess those things I'm not ready to talk to anybody about. I just write a lot about them in my journal and I guess that's kinda like talkin' about them. And, I do feel better after I write things down. That's just another form of therapy, I guess. But, you're the best kind of therapy. Talkin' with you and brushing you always makes me feel good.

"I also went to Mass with Taylor tonight before dinner. It felt good to be in a church, but I'm still not really certain where I belong. I guess as long as you have a church and you're happy with it, that makes it okay. But, there's still a lot I need to find and put together and I think I'm on the right track. One thing I do know for sure and that's that I want to be in a church on Christmas Eve or Christmas day. I certainly wouldn't feel right if I didn't attend a church service to celebrate Christmas.

"I can trust you and tell you I really am in love with Taylor and you'll keep my secret 'til I'm ready to tell her. You know that makes you the other woman in my life, but that doesn't mean I'm cheating on Taylor. I can love both of you and there's no need for you or her to be jealous."

Christmas shook her head up and down three times as if she understood exactly what he was saying and agreed completely. A moment later she began licking his left hand and continued for almost a full minute.

"I appreciate the bath, but I did shower earlier this evening." He rubbed his hand up and down her face and said, "Well, girl, it's time for you to go to bed. Get in your house."

She turned went into her stall, closed the gate and waited for her goodnight kiss.

He kissed her on the nose and said, "Goodnight, my beautiful princess."

***

Steve Whitfield opened the front door, walked into the house and saw Rose seated in the living room.

"I didn't expect to find you waiting here," he said as he took off his coat.

"I hadn't planned on it, but I thought there was something we should chat about."

He hung up his coat. "Nothing serious, I hope."

She smiled. "Well, yes and no."

"Oh, mysterious." He smiled. "Care for a drink while we have this serious or not so serious talk?"

"I'll have my usual."

"Coming right up," he said and went to the liquor cabinet in the dining room.

Steve poured a single shot of 18-year-old Macallan Scotch Whisky for her and a double for himself. A moment later he placed her glass on the coffee table in front of her and he sat down in his tan leather recliner.

He took a sip of his drink and said, "What's this serious or not serious topic we should chat about?"

"Steven, our daughter's in love."

He nodded. "With Jackson, right?"

"Yes. But you don't seem at all surprised."

"Rose, I've noticed a big difference in Taylor since he tossed her backside in the horse trough." He laughed. "She deserved that as much as you deserved being locked in that closet years ago."

"Oh, I told her about that."

"All of it?"

"Well, yes, Steven. There was no reason to leave out any of the intimate details. And, what's going on here is very close to a carbon copy of what happened between us."

"So, she told you she was in love with Jackson?

"No, not at first." She took a sip of her scotch. But, in the end there was no question as to how she felt about Jackson."

He nodded. "How do you feel about it, Rose?"

She took a breath and said, "At first I didn't care for Jackson. I think his throwing her in the horse trough had a lot to do with that. But I believe Jackson is a truly good man and I'm certain he's in love with Taylor. He's everything she wasn't looking for." She lowered her head and smiled. "Just like you were to me."

"Well, we turned out to be a very good match. Wouldn't you agree?"

"Goodness, I'd never disagree with that. Yet, it's so hard to believe that their following an almost identical course to the path we traveled in those early days."

"Like mother, like daughter. And, in this instance I think it's a good thing." He took a sip of his drink, sat the glass down and said. "Now, I am aware that Jackson has some problems, but nothing that should interfere with the way he feels about Taylor. He's confided in me about a few things and I promised I'd keep them between us until he's had time to work things out."

"Steven, are you completely comfortable with the idea of Jackson and Taylor possibly marrying sometime in the future?"

"Rose, I've liked Jackson from the first moment I saw him. He'd be a perfect match for Taylor." He shook his head and smiled. "And, I think she knew she met her match when she ended up in the horse trough."

"Oh, Steven, I was so furious about that."

"I know you were. But I knew when she blurted out what happened that she was about to travel down a very new and very different road. I saw us the first day we met."

"Oh, my, that seems so long ago and yet at times it feels like it was only yesterday."

"Yes, sir. There you were snapping orders at everybody, tellin' them to carry your bags and to be careful. I laughed and you yelled at me to open the door for you. And I said, 'look you snot nosed, spoiled brat, open it yourself'."

She laughed. "I opened the door and found the love of my life."

"Well, Rose, I'm gonna pray that Taylor and Jackson do end up marrying. When I see them together, I can feel something very special between them. They haven't put it all together yet, but I believe in time they'll find it."

"It would be so beautiful if they could find it by Christmas. Love is the absolute perfect Christmas gift."

***

Late Sunday afternoon Taylor sat down at the table in Diane Wilson's kitchen. Soon she was staring into a glass of Chianti and wondering where to begin.

Diane, however, opened the conversation. "I know you have something on your mind you want to talk about and I believe I know what it is."

"Is it that obvious to you too?"

Diane smiled. "Oh, yes. My best friend's in love."

"I've tried to tell myself it can't be true, but I know in my heart I'm head over heels in love with Jackson."

"Well, if it will make it any easier for you, I can assure you he's in love with you."

Taylor shook her head. "How can you be so sure?"

"I pushed for that horseback ride with him for a reason. I was certain you were in love with him and I was reasonably sure he was in love with you. Well, while I had my arms wrapped around him, I tried to press him for a date. I threw more than enough hints and a direct push or two and he was having none of it. He had a way out of every trap I tried to spring."

"So, that makes you think he's in love with me?"

Diane smiled again. "Taylor, I see the way he looks at you. You might miss it, but I haven't missed it and I'm sure a few others have seen it as well."

She nodded. "My mother certainly has."

"How does she feel about it?"

Taylor laughed. "Well, after my first meeting Jackson, Mom was screaming for him to be fired and thrown out of the house."

"Why?"

She took a sip of her wine and said, "I don't know if you'll believe this or not. But when I first met Jackson, he picked me up and threw me in a horse trough."

Diane burst out laughing, but finally said, "Really?"

"Yes, and I know I asked for it." She went on and told the tale of the water trough and other barn adventures and how Jackson could slice her with a verbal barb one minute and make her laugh the next.

"Oh, my, he's a whole different breed of animal than any of the others you've dated."

She again shook her head. "Yes, he is. It's so crazy how all of this began. He rescued a horse by taking her from Bob Swanson and Dad brought Jackson and the horse home with him. I swear I think Dad knew that, somehow, I'd fall in love with Jackson and I'm sure that's what he's wanted all along. Dad doesn't just like Jackson he respects him. He admires him." She took another sip of Chianti. "That's another thing, Dad has gone out of his way to put Jackson and I together. He always seems to have a project of some sort and before I know it, he's managed to pass it on to Jackson and me."

"Taylor, I've known your father for as long as I've known you. He's always been very protective of you, whether you saw it or not. If he trusts Jackson enough to practically push you into his arms, it tells me he sees him as a trustworthy and honorable man."

They talked for another hour and Diane suggested Taylor stay and have dinner with her. But, the idea of preparing a meal rather quickly gave way to a call out for pizza. So, it was pizza with pepperoni, sausage and mushrooms and the remainder of the Chianti that completed the evening's menu.

***

When Taylor arrived home, she saw the lights on in the barn and knew Jackson had to be there. As she began walking toward the barn, she noticed the first snowflakes falling and wondered if it was going to snow all night.

She went into the barn, but didn't see Jackson. She was about to turn out the lights when she thought he might be in the storage barn. As she neared the door to the other barn, she could hear the sounds of the thump, thump, thumping against the heavy bag.

She very quietly opened the door, stepped inside and eased it shut. She watched him relentlessly attack the bag, landing blow upon blow against the rough canvas surface. She slowly moved closer and saw that same burning rage she'd noticed the very first time she saw him working the heavy bag.

She didn't say a word or try to interrupt him in any way. She thought it was best to let him continue his attack until he was ready to stop and acknowledge her presence.

At last he ceased his assault with a one, two, three flurry and stepped back. He took a deep breath, exhaled sharply and wiped the sweat from his brow. He turned and looked at Taylor, but didn't say a word.

She walked directly to him, stopping only a step or two away and looking into his eyes. She stood silent for a few moments as she continued looking into his eyes. Yet, without shifting her glance, she could clearly see the scar on his left shoulder.

Taylor moved a little closer, never taking her eyes from his. "If only you'd open that door to me, I'd gladly fight your nightmares with you." She placed her right index finger to her lips, reached out and placed it against his scar. "And if you'd ask, I'd do my best to kiss away every scar."

When he tried to speak, she quickly pressed her finger to his lips, turned and walked away.

As the door closed, he whispered, "Jackson, you'd better find those answers you're lookin' for and fast."

Fourteen

Once again, Taylor sat alone in her room staring at her image in the mirror. *Taylor Whitfield,* she thought, *I don't believe what you just did. Where did you find the nerve to walk right up to Jackson and say the things you said? That's the boldest thing you've ever done. I can ask myself why, but I know why. I'm truly in love with Jackson.*

Beginning in college I set out to find Mr. Right. Mr. Perfect. I had this tremendous picture of my dream husband, perfect in every way, a man who would bow to my every wish. He had just the right job, making lots of money and he was handsome and loving and he would be there whenever I needed him, whenever I wanted him.

Jackson Riley walks into my life and he is absolutely nothing like my dream lover. He stands up to me immediately and throws me in a water trough. He makes me so mad I could scream and then makes me laugh. Oh, he's handsome, but not like Mr. Perfect. He's a rough and rugged handsome. He's so strong, but not just in a physical way. He has a confidence in his ability to do things and... She paused and smiled. *And he has this animal magnetism and, oh my, that charm can capture adults, children and every creature in the animal world. Yet, it's almost like he doesn't know or even care that he possesses such a gift.*

Everything that I see in him I never saw in my search for my version of the perfect husband. Now I wonder if I fell in love with him because he isn't the man I saw in my future. And, being honest with myself, how would a life with Mr. Everything really be? While being honest, did Jackson steal my heart the day we met and I just didn't know it? Or would that be, didn't want to admit it?

Well, after listening to Long Shot, I was wondering if he was my shot at love. So, here I am thinking, am I his Long Shot at love? Well, Jackson Riley, just like the song says "I'm gonna get to you the way you get to me" and you can count on it. Like mom said to dad, "I've been in love with you forever and I'm gonna marry you." You just don't know it yet.

***

Jackson left the storage barn after cooling down and went to give Christmas her goodnight kiss. He opened the door and her head immediately popped over her stall gate as though she knew he'd be coming by to see her.

He walked to the gate and gently ran his hand up and down her face before giving her a kiss on the nose. He put his hands on the sides of her face and softly rubbed and scratched and the look in her eyes said she was happy.

"Somehow, whatever the future holds, I believe you're the key that unlocks and opens the door. You're special in so many ways, but I can't help but feel you have a secret and I just don't know what it is yet."

He kissed her again. "Goodnight, beautiful."

A few minutes later he was sitting alone in the kitchen and sipping a cold bottle of Coors. As he slowly drank his beer, he was thinking about what Taylor had said at the barn. Her words were as clear now as they were then.

And I just hafta open the door and let her in. It all sounds so simple and I still can't do it.

He showered, turned on the computer and continued his hunt for his mother. His search, at times, seemed hopeless, but he refused to give up. He spent over an hour looking through the profiles of a dozen women named Mary Barton, but again his search failed. At one point he'd even taken a faded photograph from his wallet to compare facial features to one of the women, but she wasn't the Mary Barton he hoped to find.

He finally shut down the computer and went to sleep. In his dreams Taylor called to him and asked him to open the door to his heart and let her in. As he was reaching for her to surrender, the alarm clock played a cruel joke.

He dressed and went to the kitchen where he drank a glass of orange juice and a glass of water. He put on his down jacket and the heavy watch cap and opened the door. The four-degree temperature slapped him in the face and he laughed saying, "Good morning to you too."

He completed his morning chores and returned to the house where he found Taylor waiting. She'd decided the moment she woke up that she was going to pretend that nothing happened the night before.

She immediately went on the offensive, saying, "I was gonna fix breakfast for you, but I'm not sure I could cook that much food at one time. So, you can treat me to breakfast."

"Is that right?"

"Yes. Now get a shower and let's go. I'm hungry."

He shook his head and laughed. "Feeling a little wild and daring this morning?"

"If you don't start moving, I'll get the riding crop and show you wild and daring."

He looked at her very impish smile and said, "Yeah. Well it sounds like you're askin' for another trip to the horse trough. Keep it up and we'll see how wild and daring a four-degree dip can be."

"Well, this time I'll fight back."

"I seem to remember you fighting back, but you ended up in the trough anyway."

"I wasn't really fighting, I let you throw me in the trough."

He laughed and went to his room to shower and change.

When they arrived at the diner it seemed as though Barb had been waiting for them. She already had two menus in hand and was turning to take them to a table as soon as they passed through the door.

"So, what have you love birds battled over this morning?

"She threatened to beat me with a riding crop," Jackson said, pointing to Taylor.

"Ha. You'd probably enjoy it."

Taylor quickly lowered her head, but it was impossible to hide the dark crimson that colored her face.

"My, my," Barb said with a little chuckle. "I must've opened the naughty door." She quickly changed the topic, saying, "I guess you really don't need the menus. I'm sure you'll have the usual."

Jackson nodded. "Yes, and no smart comments with it."

"If I stop the comments, you'll think I'm sick."

He laughed. "Hey, I already think you're sick... mentally."

She smiled and walked to the kitchen. A moment later she returned to the table with coffee and orange juice for them. As she put the cups down, she said, "Anything special on the schedule this week?"

"Wednesday, Jackson and I are gonna go pick out the family Christmas tree and cut it down. Then we'll decorate it later that day."

Barb smiled. "Now, that's something I'd love to see. I bet that'll be an adventure worthy of news coverage."

***

Wednesday morning dawned with a cold wind, a temperature of five degrees and a threat of snow later in the day. Jackson was out before dawn, however, and taking care of morning chores.

Naturally, they began with a kiss for Christmas and then he

answered the demands of the other horses. They whinnied and a few snorted, encouraging him to hurry with their morning feeding.

"Okay, boys and girls, I can only take care of one of you at a time. I promise I won't cheat anybody and you'll all get an extra treat of a peppermint snack."

It didn't take long for him to feed them, but the biggest chore was breaking the ice off the outdoor water troughs. Mr. Whitfield said he was going to replace the old troughs with newer ones, which would offer heating options for the winter months.

When he walked back into the barn, he found a duo of dogs and a trio cats sitting side-by-side glaring at him. He stopped and raised his hands in the air as if surrendering to them.

"Okay. I'm sorry. I should've fed you first," he said as he retreated to the tack room to fill their food bowls.

He was still back at the house in record time and preparing to go tree hunting. After he changed clothes, Taylor surprised him, having a bow saw in hand and anxious to begin the search.

"Breakfast, first," he said with a smile.

"Good idea." She said, opening the door. "I don't want you dumpster diving at the tree farm."

He shook his head. "I have a feelin' this is gonna be a very interesting day."

Barb again greeted them at the door and led them to a table where two coffees and two glasses of orange juice were already in place. She didn't bother waiting for them to order, knowing they were like hitting a replay button when it came to what they wanted for breakfast.

When Barb headed for the kitchen, Jackson said, "You know, I really think we should fool her one morning and order something different."

"You're bad."

With breakfast over, they were in the truck and driving to the tree farm. Taylor brought along a few Christmas CDs and soon had

Silent Night playing. She began singing, adding her voice to Bing Crosby's and seemingly becoming lost in the old Christmas Carol.

When the carol ended, Jackson said, "You have a beautiful singing voice."

"You're joking, of course."

"No, I'm not. You really have a beautiful voice."

"Thank you for the compliment, but I don't think my voice is that good."

"We can argue about that later," he said, turning off the road and on to the lot of Garland's Christmas Tree Farm.

They selected a cart for carrying their tree back after it was cut down. They began their trek through the ankle deep fluffy, dry snow to search for the perfect tree. The wind chill made the five-degree air temperature feel like 25 below zero.

Jackson stopped and pulled a black mask out of his pocket. A moment later he was helping Taylor pull it over her head and soon only her eyes and a small portion of her nose were visible through the opening.

"Wow, I feel like a Ninja," she said. "But it's certainly a lot warmer than the stocking cap

"That's why I brought it along," he said, slipping one over his head. "Not much on looks, but great on protection."

It took about 25 minutes to find a tree that they both agreed would be a picture-perfect fit in the Whitfield home. Well, almost agreed. Taylor suddenly questioned the height, saying she thought it was much too tall.

"Taylor, it's not too tall."

"We should've brought a measuring tape."

He laughed. "A measuring tape? Just how do you think we could measure the tree? Have you stand on my shoulders?"

She was quiet for a moment. "Well, I guess I could sit on your shoulders. Then we'd have some idea about the height of the tree."

"You're kidding, right?"

"I know you're strong enough to support my weight on your shoulders. It would only take a second from that vantage point to see just how tall the tree is."

"So, you're not kidding?"

She shook her head. "No, I'm not."

"Now, before we jump into this insane idea, let me point out that the ground here is very slippery. We added to that by stompin' around and lookin' the tree over. So, if you're up there and I slip, we're both gonna end up…"

"You're not gonna slip. Now, get down and let me get on your shoulders."

He dropped to one knee muttering, "Jackson, you did some crazy things in the Corps, but I think this is gonna top them all."

"Oh, will you stop worrying? We've got this." She managed to climb on to his shoulders and said, "Okay, stand up."

He very cautiously began to stand and in a matter of seconds succeeded in gaining his feet. He stood as still as possible, but she on the other hand, was leaning first to her right and then to her left.

"Taylor, it would be a very good idea if you didn't wiggle around."

"I'm not wiggling."

"I can't believe I let you talk me into this."

She raised her right hand to try and gauge the height of the tree and was suddenly losing her balance. She grabbed his head for support.

"I can't see," he yelled. "Pull my mask up. You pushed it over my eyes."

She screamed as she completely lost her balance and began to topple backward. He attempted to grab her as she was falling from his shoulders, but lost his balance and began falling backward as well.

She screamed again as she fell between the branches of two

Douglas firs and landed in a very deep pile of snow. Jackson spun to his left and was able to catch his balance for only a second or two before he fell and landed squarely on top of her.

His mask was gone and he was looking directly into those oh so beautiful blue eyes. He took a breath and said, "Well, Little Miss I'm not wiggling, any more bright ideas?"

"You did that on purpose," she snapped, slapping him on the shoulder.

"You're right. I planned the whole thing. In fact, I've got five camera crews over there disguised as Santa's Elves and the Abominable Snowman and this will be on the six o'clock news this evening."

She ripped her mask off, but the moment she saw the smile on his face she began laughing. "I can't believe you do this to me."

"Do what?"

"Make me laugh. I mean, every time I try to be angry with you, you do something to make me laugh."

He was about to answer, but was cut off by Dan Garland, the owner of the tree farm. "Are you okay? I heard screaming."

Taylor said, "Oh, we just slipped and fell. We're fine."

He smiled and nodded. "Yes, Sir. Sure looks that way from where I'm standin'. Have fun, but be careful not to catch frostbite."

Jackson pushed himself up and offered her a hand. When she was standing, he said, "It's that tree... the one you *measured*. That's it and it's not open for discussion."

She laughed. "I'll just stand and watch you cut."

About ten minutes later, Dan Garland was placing the tree in a machine to have the loose needles shaken free. When he was sure the last loose needle had fallen off, he ran the tree through the tube for binding and wished them a very Merry Christmas.

Before leaving they purchased a new Christmas tree stand and a half-dozen evergreen wreaths. Jackson put the tree in the bed of the truck and affixed one of the wreaths to the truck's grill before they began the drive home.

"That was a lotta fun," Taylor said. "I really enjoyed that."

He nodded. "You're right. Even though you insisted on snow diving, it was fun. I'd love to do it again…with you."

She looked over at him. "We won't be able to do it again 'til next Christmas."

"That's okay," he said with a shrug. "I can wait."

Jackson caught her completely off guard with his comment and she was so taken by what he said, she couldn't answer.

But, he saved her from stumbling through a reply that she was certain would have made no sense by saying, "Coffee?"

"Yes. Please."

He turned off the road, pulled into a parking space. "You can stay in the truck and keep warm. I'll get it."

"They have a drive-thru, you know."

"I hate those things. Too impersonal."

She smiled and thought, *of course they are. But you're not. You prefer face to face contact and talking with the counter girl. And no doubt she loves it when you smile and share a few casual words with her. But, that's what makes you special.*

He returned and handed her a cup and said, "Time to get this tree home and get everything ready to decorate it."

"I thought we could do that after dinner this evening. I'm not sure if mom or dad will wanna help."

"Good idea. We wouldn't wanna cheat them out of the fun of decorating the Christmas tree." He chuckled. "If it's as much of an adventure decorating it as it was cuttin' it down, it could be a wild evening and I'm sure they wouldn't wanna miss that."

"Oh, there shouldn't be any problem at all decorating it."

"Really? I'll believe that when we've finished and the house is still standing."

***

Evening chores at the barn were over and it was time for

dinner. Juanita had prepared tuna steaks, white rice and mixed vegetables for the evening meal and pumpkin pie for dessert.

Taylor was anxious to begin decorating the tree, but was quickly reminded that it had to be put up first. Then she urged everyone to hurry and finish their meal, but dad told her to settle down and wait.

"Taylor, there'll be ample time to decorate the tree," her mother said. "Have a slice of pie and the time will pass so much quicker."

And, it wasn't long before Taylor and Jackson were opening the front door and dragging the tree inside. That's when the first discussion of the evening began.

"We should put the tree up right here against this wall," she said, looking at Jackson and pointing to the wall between the kitchen door and the entrance archway.

"Against the wall? That's crazy. It should go in the center of the room," he said.

"It'll take up too much room."

"Will you take a good look at the size of these rooms? This is a big open space. You could put this tree and a hundred people in here and still have room."

She shook her head. "No, absolutely not. It should go there against the wall."

"Okay, Miss Up Against the Wall, tell me why somebody put two perfectly placed electrical outlets in the floor, both of which are there to accommodate electric plugs. You know, the kind that run from the Christmas tree lights?"

"I don't care. The tree should be against that wall."

"Since, we can't agree, let's flip a coin. The winner picks the spot for the tree."

"That's fine with me."

Jackson took a quarter from his pocket. "Okay, you call it."

"Heads," she said as he flipped the coin in the air.

He allowed the coin to land on the floor and after a bounce and a few spins it dropped tails up.

"You cheated."

"Cheated? How can I cheat flippin' a coin?"

"I don't know, but you did."

He handed her the quarter. "Okay, let's try it again. You flip and I'll even let you call it."

"That sounds fair." She took the coin, flipped it in the air and called, "Tails."

It struck the floor, spun slowly and fell heads up.

Jackson smiled. "I win. The tree goes in the center of the room."

Her father got up from his recliner and started for the kitchen. "Rose, I'm gonna fix some popcorn and grab a beer. Can I get you anything?"

"Are we watching television?"

He laughed. "Oh, no. I'm gonna watch Taylor and Jackson put the tree up and decorate it. Nothing on TV can come close to the entertainment we're about to have here."

She smiled. "A glass of red wine."

"Well, the way this has started out, you might want the whole bottle."

Taylor reluctantly gave in and put the Christmas tree stand in the center of the floor between the electrical outlets. Jackson picked up the tree, maneuvered it in place and lowered it on the center peg. He let go of the tree and smiled when he saw that it was standing flawlessly straight. Next, he picked up a pair of scissors and began cutting the netting from around the tree. The limbs flowed out to the sides, opening to reveal a magnificent Douglas Fir.

He looked at Taylor. So, what do you think?"

"It's really a beautiful tree. And… And, I admit it does look good in the center of the room."

"Okay. This is my first time decorating a Christmas tree, so where do we start?"

"Let's bring the ladder in and put the star on top of the tree."

"Shouldn't an angel be on top of the tree?"

Steve glanced at Rose. "I might hafta go pop another bag of popcorn."

Taylor looked at Jackson and crossed her arms. "I think it should be a star."

"Okay. Let's flip for it."

She put her hands on her hips. "Oh, no. We're not gonna have another coin toss. You'd just cheat again."

He smiled at her. "I got the tree in the center of the room, so I guess you get the star on top of the tree."

"Oh... you... you make me crazy." She pointed to the front door. "Go get the ladder."

Within a minute he had retrieved the ladder and placed it by the tree. "Do you want me to put the star on the tree?"

"No," she said. "I'll do it."

He laughed. "Let's not have a repeat of this morning."

"What happened this morning?" Steve said, getting out of his chair and walking close to the tree.

"Nothing," Taylor said. "Nothing at all."

Steve looked at Jackson. "I know this has to be a good story. So you tell it."

"Don't you dare," Taylor blurted.

It was too late. Jackson was already relating the tale of the great Christmas Tree Caper. When he reached the part where Taylor pushed his mask over his eyes, Rose was doubled over laughing. By the time he was telling of their fall into the snow pile, Rose was up and hurrying out of the room.

She managed to blurt, "I'm about to pee my pants."

Steve was laughing, Jackson was chuckling, Rose closed the hallway bathroom door and Taylor was pretending she was angry.

Her anger ruse fell apart when she began laughing. "Okay, I

admit it was funny. I didn't think so at first though."

Order was restored and Taylor climbed the ladder, put the star atop the tree and made it down without falling. Then she and Jackson began putting the lights on the tree and, working together, strung 750 lights without arguing or knocking the tree over.

They paused long enough for a glass of water and went back to work placing the other decorations. They alternated going up and down the ladder as they moved around the tree to complete trimming the top.

Steve and Rose glanced over at each other and smiled as they watched Taylor and Jackson working side by side as they hung the ornaments and placed the tinsel on the tree. There was something else they saw in their daughter and the young man who seemed to come out of nowhere and into their lives. They were truly enjoying themselves as they worked. They were laughing, smiling and, of course, they made time for a bit of verbal jousting.

At last the Christmas tree was decorated and they stepped back to admire their work. They nodded, smiled and a high-five seemed in order.

"Okay," Taylor said. "Time to see the Whitfield Family Christmas tree in all its splendor. Turn out the lights first."

A moment later Taylor flipped the light switch on one side of the tree, while Jackson turned on the lights from the opposite side.

Rose stood up and said, "Oh, my. That's beautiful."

"Wow! That's some tree," Steve said.

Jackson and Taylor walked to the front window and looked at the tree. They were standing side by side and Taylor moved a little closer and slipped her hand into his. He squeezed gently, looked at her and smiled.

"We make a good team," he said, as he squeezed her hand just a little tighter.

"Yes, we do," she whispered.

Rose took Steve by the arm and smiled. "Well, I've certainly grown to like that young man and I believe Taylor's found the man she's been looking for."

Steve nodded. "You're right and I bet she didn't interview him for the position."

Fifteen

Jackson was up and out of the house early as usual and on his way to the barn. He was smiling before he opened the door, knowing he was about to get his normal demands from horses, dogs and cats.

This morning he started the feeding ritual with the dogs and cats, which was greeted with a chorus of rather loud objections from the equine section.

He laughed as he began his trek from stall to stall, chatting with horses and ponies as he dumped their morning grain ration into their pails. He received a few appreciative nickers and whinnies as he made his rounds and happily acknowledged their thanks.

He finally reached Christmas's stall and she knew it was time for her good morning kiss. He kissed her nose opened the gate, went in and filled her grain bucket.

"You hafta stay in this morning, girl. Gary's gonna stop by and check the shoe on your right front hoof. I think's it a little loose and I wanna make sure it's snug.

While she was eating, he called the diner, spoke to Barb and placed a carry out order for Jose, George and himself. He told her he'd be by in an hour to pick it up.

When he hung up it was time to take the horses out to the

pastures. He began with those he fed first and worked his way to Comet and Cupid.

He returned to the barn just as Jose and George arrived and he told them he was off to pick up breakfast for them. They offered a quick thank you and began cleaning stalls.

Barb had his arrival timed to the second. When she spotted his truck turning on to the lot, she hurried to the kitchen and picked up his order. She was already at the cash register ringing up the total when he walked in.

"Now that's what I call service," he said, passing the exact amount to her for the meal and a separate pass for her tip.

"How was the Christmas tree search?"

He laughed. "That's a story that'll take a little time to tell. Next trip, remind me."

"Count on that," she said, smiling. "I can't wait."

"Probably see you in the morning."

He walked to the truck and headed back to the farm. On the way he listened to Christmas Carols and every now and then he'd sing along.

I feel better about this Christmas. And more than I've ever felt about any other, but there's still something missing. I guess a little prayer wouldn't hurt. Maybe there's one for findin' the right answers.

Jackson called for a breakfast break when he arrived at the barn. A few minutes later he was sitting on a saddle in the tack room having breakfast with Jose and George. They laughed and joked as they ate, and a few comments were made about George and his love life. He tried to brush off the banter, but finally confessed that he was enjoying his new relationship.

Gary arrived shortly after eight and Jackson opened the stall gate and brought Christmas out.

Gary smiled. "I thought you would've trained her to open that by now."

"I thought about it, but decided against it after I found out she has her heart set on a romance with Bronson."

Gary nodded. "They'd probably make a mighty fine colt together."

"I have no doubt about that. But I'd rather wait for a while and see how things go before I think about her lettin' her have her fantasy fling."

They talked while Gary worked and refitted her shoe. When he finished, Jackson paid him for his work and then gave him a gift certificate to his favorite seafood restaurant.

"You didn't hafta do that," he said, shaking his head.

"Gary, not that I've been here that long, but you always go the extra mile for us around here. A little appreciation bonus is well deserved."

"Like I said, you didn't hafta do it, but thank you"

"Enjoy a night out."

He laughed. "I'll see if I can latch on to some fine lookin' honey, preferably a rich and lonely one, and make a night of it."

Just as Gary left, Steve Whitfield entered the barn and called Jackson over.

"Yes, Sir, Mr. Whitfield, what's up?"

"I thought you should be the first to know, Senator Blake did it. He pulled all the right strings and Gunnery Sergeant Davidson's gonna make it home for Christmas."

"That's great," he said with a big smile. "Any idea when he'll get in?"

"If all goes according to what John told me, his flight will land at 7:00 AM on Christmas Eve."

"What's the plan to get Helen and Addie to the hotel and what hotel are you thinkin' about?"

"I've got a call in to the Cedar Towers Hotel. It's about a twenty-minute drive from the airport. As far as gettin' Helen and Addie there, I'm gonna call Helen's sister, Marie, and fill her in on all the details. I'm sure she'll jump at the opportunity to help when she finds out what we're doin'."

"You still want me to meet Gunny Davidson and escort him to the hotel?"

"Absolutely."

He smiled. "I'm lookin' forward to it and I'm sure Taylor's gonna help. She'll enjoy his homecoming."

"Now, on another note," Steve said. "I found out you donated a very substantial amount of money to help out a few needy families and their children."

"Uh... I thought that was supposed to be kept a secret."

Steve nodded. "Well, I have what you might call 'ears to the ground' all over Cedar Falls. So, somebody whispered to me what you'd done, but only to me. What you gave amounts to almost your entire earnings here."

Jackson shook his head. "Well, I got a very nice separation packet when I left the Corps. So, it wasn't like I didn't have money to give."

"Well, that was a very good thing you did. So, I added some to your donation and those families are gonna get extra in the food and clothing line."

"That's very generous of you, Sir."

"Jackson, I can afford to be generous. I'm not so sure about you though."

"Mr. Whitfield, I didn't have much of anything when I was growin' up. So, I'm kinda used to my pockets not being filled to the brim. And my Christmases were always a disaster at home and when I was shipped off to military school, they weren't much better. I just wanted to make sure a few families and their children had a little something nice for Christmas... something that might give a bit of happiness to the day."

"I certainly admire what you did and I have a feelin' you don't want anybody else to know about it."

"No, Sir. I especially don't want any publicity for what I did. I'd just like to be happy for those families and be left alone."

Steve put his hand on his shoulder. "Your secret's safe with me."

Jackson nodded. "Thank you. Oh, by the way, I hear we're gonna get some more snow."

"Last weather report I heard said we could get up to a foot before it stops."

He laughed. "Never believe what the weatherman tells you. I think the weathermen and women just want you to be happy if you only get a foot of snow."

Steve laughed and said, "You're probably right."

Jackson went back to the tack room and picked up the cup of French Fries Barb had slipped in with his order. He plucked one from the cup, took a bite and decided cold or not they were still very tasty.

He opened the stall gate and Christmas slowly sauntered out and stopped in front of him. A second later she eased her head closer to him and with the skill of a magician pulled the zipper of his jacket down.

He glanced down. "Hey, what kinda trick is this?"

When he looked up Christmas was holding two French Fries in her mouth. She held them momentarily as though taunting him and then casually chewed up the yummy potatoes and swallowed them.

"You thief. I hope you're proud of yourself."

She gave a little nicker and he was certain it was her way of laughing at him.

"Okay, out to the pasture."

He turned and began walking to the barn door, not bothering to put the halter or lead line on her. A moment later she was walking casually by his side as the snow began to fall. He gave her a kiss and closed the pasture gate, while she waited for him to give her another kiss.

"I shouldn't give you another smooch on the nose, but then I'd feel guilty and come back and give you one anyway."

He scratched her behind the ears for a few seconds, kissed her on the nose again and walked back to the barn.

***

Jackson returned to the house and spent another two hours on the computer searching for his mother. Yet, it seemed as though the gods of luck were intentionally blocking his efforts. He leaned back in the chair, stared up at the ceiling and muttered, "You won't beat me. I refuse to let you win."

He got up and called Sid and asked if he could stop by for a haircut. Sid told him he was open for at least the next hour and to drive in before the snowfall picked up in intensity.

When he walked out to his truck the snow was already six inches deep. He turned on the radio and waited for the weather forecast, guessing that the snow totals would be a little more than originally predicted. After what seemed like a never-ending stream of commercials for everything from razor blades to deodorant, the voice of the woman he called "Miss Cheerful" came on.

In her normal, dull monotone voice she informed listeners to prepare for at least 18 inches of snow. In addition to the snow, high winds were predicted to arrive after midnight and the temperatures would remain somewhere in the single digits, but above zero.

Jackson parked his truck on the lot beside the barbershop and walked in to a greeting of "Merry Christmas" from Sid. Just as he sat down in the chair, Sheriff Bart Jennings opened the door and stepped inside.

"Okay, Sid, you can call off the snow," the sheriff said as he hung his Stetson on the wall rack.

"Bart, I wish it was that easy."

The sheriff sat down, looked at Jackson and said, "I know you have your job application in with the State Police and you've been accepted. Now, I just found out this morning that Ben Parker's gonna retire at the end of the month, leavin' me a man short. That slot's yours if you want it."

Jackson certainly wasn't expecting a job offer while getting a haircut. He looked at Jennings and said, "You caught me off guard, Sheriff. I appreciate the offer, but I kinda had my sights set on the State Police."

"Well, why don't you think it over? Our next academy class won't start 'til mid April."

He nodded. "Let me think about it. I guess there'd be a few advantages takin' a job here."

"You'd be guaranteed you wouldn't be shipped off to some far corner of the state after the academy. You'd stay right here in Cedar Falls."

"That's sure a plus. I like Cedar Falls and the people here. I got to know a lotta the businessmen and women over the past few weeks."

Jennings smiled. "You'd have your own car or one of those new four-wheel drive SUVs we got in last month. And, your salary would be about five-thousand more than you'd be makin' with the State Police."

Jackson smiled. "Sheriff, you're runnin' a full court press on me."

"Oh, when I see a man with your background and I want him on my team, yes, sir, I run the full court press."

"And I bet you haven't played all your cards yet."

Jennings laughed. "Yeah, that's true. There's the medical benefits package, which includes dental coverage. Then there's the pension plan, very good working hours and a very favorable leave schedule."

"Anything else?"

The sheriff nodded. "Well, there's some talk around town about you and a certain young lady. Seems to me havin' her close by would be an added incentive."

"Sheriff, were you a used car salesman before you got into law enforcement?"

The three men laughed and Jennings said, "No, but that's what I was planning on after retirement."

"I have no doubt you'll be a big success."

As Jackson got out of the chair, Jennings said, "Take your time and think about my offer. I mean it. Give it some very serious thought."

"Yes, sir, I'll do that."

He wished the two men a very Merry Christmas and walked back out into the snow. The snowfall was steady and the total was rising by the hour. He figured it could be a long night for the police and road crews on the snowplows.

He drove back to the farm and decided to spend some more time with Christmas. He had little trouble coaxing her out of the pasture and she strolled along beside him into the barn.

He removed her blanket and said, "You know with this coat you have, you probably don't really need this. I mean you are one fuzzy girl."

He picked up a brush and started stroking her forelock after giving her a carrot, of course. "You know, sweetheart, I sure am happy you came into my life. You can make a difference when a few things or a lotta things seem wrong or they bother me. When I was at the military school, I was always happiest when I was around the horses. Somehow, they made all the bad things in my life seem like they weren't so bad after all. I think that's why I was always able to concentrate and study the way I should."

He gave her another carrot and began brushing her mane. "I guess I owe a lotta things in my life to horses. I got very good grades in school and I made the honor roll every grading period from sixth grade through high school. Naturally, that meant I took a lotta grief from others in my classes. They said it made me a... oh well, never mind what they said, and I was always able to put them back in their place. Now, sometimes that meant that a few of 'em, ended up with a black eye or a fat lip. But I had to make it clear that they weren't gonna dictate how things went in my life."

He paused to answer his phone, but it was a wrong number. "I know I pound on the heavy bag a lot, but nothing compares to havin' my time with you. You make my life a good place and you know my secret about the way I feel about Taylor.

"When I think about it, and I think about it a lot, I still don't know why or how I ended up stoppin' at that horse auction. Maybe it really is like Mr. Whitfield said, that it was fate or the Man up above sent me in. But, no matter the reason, I'll always be happy that I found you."

He kissed her on the nose and said, "Well, girl, I guess I'd better start gettin' the evening meal ready and bringin' everybody in. With this snow, I'm sure they won't mind."

He went about prepping the evening feeding, pouring grain into the pails and topping off water buckets. Next, came the flakes of hay for everyone and he was off to the pasture to bring them in.

He purposely saved Bronson till last and when he brought him in "Lover Boy" stopped to give a nuzzle to Christmas. When he was put in his stall, he gave a whinny and she answered.

Jackson gave all the horses a peppermint treat before feeding Rooster, Rita, Hank, Sylvester and Sylvia. He made sure to give them each a special treat as well and they rewarded him with a few quick yaps and heartfelt meows.

***

Dinner was served at five and Steve insisted they turn on the TV in the kitchen to catch the news about the weather. The snow storm was the lead story and for snow lovers the forecast was very favorable. The snowfall was expected to end by midnight with a total accumulation of twenty-inches.

Just as dessert was served an emergency broadcast captured

their attention. Two children, ages seven and five, were missing in the storm and a search was being organized immediately. A request for volunteers to aid in the search was broadcast and those wanting to assist should report to Sheriff Bart Jennings at the entrance to the Swanson Farm.

Jackson stood up. "That's not far from here. I'm gonna get dressed and go help."

"I'll call Diane and a few others and we can get food, water, coffee and hot chocolate for the volunteers," Taylor said.

"Good idea," her father said. "Your mother and I can help out with that too."

"Mr. Whitfield, take my truck," Jackson said, handing him the keys.

"How're you gonna get there?"

"On horseback. It'll be a lot easier for Christmas to move through the snow. A person trudging through a foot or move of snow and tryin' to concentrate on finding two lost kids is gonna wear out quick."

While Steve, Rose and Taylor went to pick up Diane and food supplies, Jackson dressed and headed to the barn.

He saddled Christmas after wrapping her legs with Polo wraps, although she probably didn't really need them for warmth. It was just a precaution he wanted to take. Next, he put on his backpack, which had a few candy bars, water and two wool blankets tucked inside.

Soon he was sitting astride Christmas and moving easily through the snow toward the Swanson Farm. When he arrived, he tracked down Sheriff Jennings and told him he was there to help.

Jennings pulled him aside. "It's Swanson's grandchildren who're missing. Robby, age seven and Samantha, age five. I'm tryin' to get things organized and he keeps buttin' in and screwin' things up."

"Well, I'm sure that's normal behavior for him."

"The last time Swanson saw the kids they were out here near the gate with a sled. He was on his tractor plowin' out the driveway and tryin' to keep tabs on where they were. Naturally, he got too involved plowing and when he finally realized he'd gotten pretty far away from the front gate, they were gone."

"Any idea where they might've headed?"

"I think they crossed the road and went into the woods on the other side. Swanson disagrees. He said they wouldn't cross the road because he told them never to cross it."

Jackson looked slowly around and studied the snow-covered landscape. "Well, Sheriff, I agree with you. The snow's piled up on both sides of the driveway and, here at the entrance, it has to be five feet high or higher on both sides. If they walked back toward the house, they would've passed him, but obviously they didn't. Since I don't see the sled anywhere, I'm guessing they took it with 'em."

"That's what I think too." Jennings said. "And I say they went across the road with the sled."

"Well, it's the path of least resistance. Way too tough for a seven year old and a five year old to push a sled up over those snow piles in the driveway. They might be packed solid, but they're also almost straight up. Unless they're part mountain goat, they didn't go over the piles and into the fields or woods on this side of the road."

"While Swanson's screwin' things up over here, why don't you start lookin' along the road on the other side."

"I'm on it."

'Here, take this handheld with you," Jennings said, passing a portable radio to Jackson.

"I'll stay off the radio unless I find something, Sheriff."

With that, Jackson turned Christmas around and crossed the road. He glanced back over his right shoulder and saw there were at least a hundred people waiting to begin searching. As he rode slowly along the roadside, he did see about two-dozen men tromping into the woods not far behind him. At least they were looking on the same side as he was searching.

"Okay, girl, let's see if we can find these kids." He patted her gently on the neck and scanned the roadside.

The plows had gone over the road very recently, which made the search a lot tougher. But Jackson kept scanning back and forth looking for some telltale sign that might lead him to the children. It was a gap between the trees that caused him to rein Christmas to a halt.

"The path of least resistance," he muttered. "There it is."

He patted Christmas twice on the left side of her neck and she turned left and slowly walked off the roadway. Jackson looked left and right, reining Christmas to a halt about every 25 feet to stop and listen. The pace was extremely slow, but he wanted to be sure he didn't miss a sound or possible visible clue.

He kept the radio turned down low, but could still hear the messages being transmitted. At times it sounded as though someone was countering Sheriff Jennings's directions and confusing the men and women searching. He was sure it had to be Swanson.

"Sheriff, a little duct tape would end that," he muttered as he moved on.

Jackson kept a slow, steady pace, while looking and listening for signs of Robby and Samantha. Christmas quickly proved she could sense they were on a quest and soon was stopping every 25 to 30 feet without a signal from Jackson.

He smiled and gently rubbed her neck as he said, "That's a good girl. You're much smarter than that dipstick who said you were worthless and wanted to get rid of you."

She shook her head up and down and Jackson laughed.

They continued their pace and had worked their way into the woods for almost a half-mile. Suddenly Christmas stopped and her ears stood up as she turned her head to the left. She was frozen in place and on full alert. After a few seconds she gave a quick snort.

"What is it, girl?" He looked to his left again and called out,

"Robby, Samantha can you hear me?"

Christmas took a half-dozen quick steps, stopped and, once again, she went to full alert. Her ears were straight up, her eyes wide and looking to her left. She gave a quick snort and remained alert.

Jackson called out again. "Robby, Samantha, can you hear me."

This time someone answered. The voice was barely audile, but he was certain he'd found them. He pulled his right foot from the stirrup and a moment later dropped to the snow-covered ground.

He slowly made his way off the path and went deeper into the woods. He called their names again and this time when they answered he was closer.

Although he knew he'd found Robby and Samantha, he was not going to notify Sheriff Jennings until he had them and was on his way out. He knew if he called before he was already on his way out, there'd be a stampede from the family and members of the search party.

Jackson had traveled about 30 to 40 feet off the path when he noticed movement to his right. He paused, pulled a small flashlight from his pocket and shined the beam in the direction of the motion. Suddenly, two small heads popped out from inside an old tree.

He nodded and smiled. They were smart enough to seek shelter in a tree that had long ago surrendered its life to the forces of nature. As time passed, the old tree had decayed from the inside out and provided a perfect refuge for the children.

In a matter of seconds, he was dropping to one knee in front of them. "Hello, Robby, hello, Samantha, I'm Jackson. I guess you must be a little hungry and thirsty."

They nodded and said, "Yes."

He removed two bottles of water from his backpack, opened them and passed one to each of them. He waited for them to take a drink and said, "How would you like a candy bar?"

Of course, they eagerly answered, "Yes" to that question as

well.

"Well, I have Snickers bars, Three Musketeers bars and some Milky Way bars. Which one do you want?"

Samantha said, "Three Musketeers."

"I want a Snickers bar," Robby said.

He passed them their candy bars and after they'd eaten about half, he said, "Okay, let's go and get you home."

He guided them out of the woods and to the path where they found Christmas waiting patiently. He pulled the blankets from the backpack and draped them over Christmas just to the front of the saddle horn.

Next, he mounted up and said, "Robby, give me your hand and I'll pull you up." Seconds later Robby was sitting behind him. Jackson took one of the blankets, passed it to Robby and told him to wrap it around his shoulders.

"Okay, Samantha, your turn," he said, reaching down to her.

He effortlessly hoisted her from the ground and soon she was wrapped in the other blanket and he clutched her close with his left arm. He wrapped the reins loosely around the saddle horn and gave Christmas two pats on the left side of her neck. As she began to turn, he patted her until she was turned around and facing in the direction of the roadway.

Christmas walked slowly through the snow, which was now at least 16 inches deep, and her laid-back gait suggested that she was aware that their mission was almost completed.

Jackson pulled the radio from his right coat pocket and keyed the mic. "Sheriff Jennings?"

"Jackson?"

"Yes, Sir. I have Robby and Samantha. They're okay."

"Where are you?"

"I'll be comin' outta the woods from the opposite side of the road. Should be there in a minute or two."

On the way out, Robby told Jackson what had happened and

how they managed to find the old hollow tree and take shelter.

By the time Jackson, Christmas, Robby and Samantha broke from the tree line, the road was filled with a mass of humanity. From the Sheriff and his deputies, to the entire Swanson family, members of the search party and, of course, the media.

Questions were being fired at Jackson from every imaginable direction and chaos dominated until Sheriff Jennings stepped up and blew his whistle.

Jackson passed the children down as the Swanson family and a medical team rushed forward.

Bob Swanson looked up at Jackson. "Uh… I don't know how to thank you for savin' my grandchildren."

Jackson shook his head. "Don't thank me. Thank this very beautiful and intelligent horse. She alerted and showed we where they were."

"Well, I'm gonna make sure you get a nice reward for this," Swanson said, ensuring that the TV microphones were in range to pick up his heartfelt gratitude. "You just name it."

Jackson stared down at him. "Really?"

"My word on that. You just name it."

Jackson smiled. "So, if I tell you to write out a nice fat check in the amount of… oh, say a hundred thousand dollars, you'll do it without question."

Swanson knew the young man had very shrewdly backed him into a corner. It was pay up or look like a fool. "Uh… well, I gave you my word. I'll stand by it."

"Mr. Swanson, I don't want the money for myself. I'd like you to donate half to the Cedar Falls Horse Rescue and the other half to an organization that uses horses to work with returning veterans suffering from PTSD." He leaned down and said, "At least your generosity's gonna get you a nice tax write-off."

"You're a lot smarter than I gave you credit for."

He nodded. "The next time you wanna gamble, pick a man

who won't call your bluff."

When Swanson walked away, Jackson was bombarded with questions from the media.

He raised a hand and calmly said, "Robby, is the real hero in this story. You should interview him. He's a very smart little boy. He watched a survival show on TV, paid very close attention and knew exactly what to do when he and Samantha got lost."

He picked up the reins and moved Christmas slowly through the crowd, refusing to answer any more questions from the press. He paused long enough to give Sheriff Jennings the radio and told him he'd be in touch later.

He worked his way around everybody until he located Taylor and her parents. He pulled off the backpack and asked Mr. Whitfield to toss it in his truck.

He looked at Taylor and smiled. "If you're lost, I can help you find your way home."

She held out her hands. "I'm lost."

He pulled his left foot from the stirrup and took Taylor's right hand. She put her left foot in the stirrup and a moment later was seated behind Jackson and wrapping her arms around him.

Diane looked at the Whitfields. "Oh, she's not lost. For the first time in her life, she's really in love and just hasn't figured out how to deal with it."

Sixteen

By now the media teams had swarmed around the medics and the ambulance and were bombarding Robby with questions. It was a surprise to everyone, but Robby fielded the questions as though he'd been standing in the public eye since birth.

He told everyone that he and Samantha had crossed the road to find a better place to sleigh ride. While searching, they found a path, left their sleigh by a tree and started into the woods. After walking for a while, they left the path and went into the woods. With the snow falling harder they became confused and weren't sure of the way out.

Robby said he saw the old tree and knew if they went into the space they could stay warm. But before they took shelter, he broke some of the old bark from the tree and put it inside so they could stand on it. He told reporters he remembered that from a TV survival show he watched and knew the bark would insulate them from the cold ground.

The interview concluded when Robby told reporters how Jackson found them and gave them water and a candy bar. Then he told of their ride out and said, "It's really cool. Mr. Jackson calls his horse Christmas."

***

Jackson reined Christmas to a halt at the front steps of the house and helped Taylor down.

She looked up at him, smiled and said, "Thank you, kind sir, for rescuing me and showing me the way home."

He gave a slight bow. "Well, ma'am it's always a pleasure to rescue a damsel in distress."

"Care for a sandwich when you come back from the barn?"

He nodded. "That would be great. I worked up an appetite out there in the snow."

She laughed. "Personally, I believe you work up an appetite while eating."

"I bet you've been savin' that one up for a while."

"I'll meet you in the kitchen."

A few minutes later he removed the saddle, reins and Polo wrap from Christmas and began brushing her down. "You were the real hero out there, sweetheart. You found those kids and saved their lives."

He paused and kissed her on the nose. He brushed her down and put on her blanket, said goodnight and she went to her stall. He gave her a little extra grain before kissing her again and closing the stall gate.

When he reached the kitchen, he stopped in the doorway and said, "Wow! If that tastes as good as the aroma, I might force myself to eat two sandwiches."

"Ha. You mean two dozen, don't you?" Taylor shot back as he sat down. "And when did you ever have to force yourself to eat?"

"Huuumm… I'd hafta think about that."

While they were out with the search party, Juanita had baked a ham. Now, still piping hot she put it on the kitchen table with a loaf of rye bread, a loaf of white and a loaf of whole wheat bread. She also put out mustard, mayonnaise, lettuce, tomatoes and pickles.

Jackson placed four slices of ham between two pieces of rye bread and took a bite of his sandwich.

Taylor gave him a quizzical look. "Aren't you gonna put any mustard or mayo on your sandwich."

"Never when it's hot. Anything besides the bread would take away from the taste of the ham. Mustard, mayo or anything else is only used when ham is cold. Then they enhance the flavor."

Taylor laughed. "I guess I should've known that you'd know best how to eat a ham sandwich. Of course, with your love of food, I'm sure you'd know best how to eat anything."

"Yes, and I can cook too."

She sat back and stared at him. "Oh, you cannot. You're just teasing."

"No, I'm not."

"Okay, what can you cook? A hard-boiled egg?"

He put down his sandwich. "That's it. I'll fix dinner for all of us tomorrow evening."

"Great," she laughed. "Hard-boiled eggs and lettuce."

"And I suppose you're a master chef?"

"I can cook better than you."

"Well, Chef Taylor, we'll cook dinner together. The menu is Rib Eye Steak, sautéed mushrooms and twice baked potato. You do the vegetable cooking, and I'll grill the steaks."

She smiled. "Wow, we're gonna have scorched rubber for dinner."

"Oh, you're in for a big surprise." He looked at Juanita. "I think you should have tomorrow night off from your cooking chores. But I want you to have dinner with us and you can't help Taylor."

She laughed. "Thank you. I think I'm going to enjoy this very much."

"First thing in the morning, I'm off to the meat locker for steaks," he said, reaching for his sandwich. "I'd say an inch and a half thick should be satisfactory."

The verbal duel over who had the better cooking skills went on for another half-hour. When the sparring ended nothing had been settled and it was obvious the preparation of tomorrow's evening meal would be a battle for chef supremacy.

Jackson stood up. "First thing in the morning, after the barn chores and breakfast, we'll pick up steaks and veggies for the War of the Chefs."

"Oh, I can't wait," Taylor said with a big smile.

By morning the snow had stopped and the wind diminished to a whisper. Snowplows had been out all night and the main roads were open. Radio and TV broadcasts said most businesses would be open as usual, but schools were closed.

The first stop after barn chores was the Cedar Falls Diner and a hearty breakfast.

Barb started the morning by saying, "Well, Jackson, you are definitely becoming quite the celebrity around town."

"I'd prefer not to be a celebrity around Cedar Falls or any other town."

"Well, I think those kids wouldn't have survived if it wasn't for you. You deserve a lotta praise and thanks for what you did."

"The only reward and thanks I care about is the lives of those kids. They survived and that's all that matters to me. Besides, it was my horse, Christmas, that alerted me to where they were. So she's the one who deserves all the praise and thanks."

With that Barb switched gears and quickly reminded Jackson he had to tell her of the Great Christmas Tree Caper.

Over Taylor's obviously feigned objections, Jackson related the tale of their adventure at the Garland Tree Farm. Barb, of course, found the story more than a little amusing and said it was too bad the escapade hadn't been filmed.

The next stop after breakfast was the grocery store to pick up vegetables, various seasonings and a few essential items to prep the veggies.

Then it was off to the meat locker where Roland happily cut the Rib Eye steaks to order after hearing of the soon to come cook off challenge.

Once back at the Whitfield home, Jackson seasoned and wrapped the steaks before placing them in the refrigerator. From the kitchen he went to the fireplace where he arranged the mesquite wood and kindling to allow for maximum oxygen to ensure a quick starting, hot fire.

Satisfied that his preparatory work was complete, he dressed appropriately and returned to the barn. The horses would be returned to their stalls because of the extreme cold and he would spend time with Christmas.

She followed him into the indoor arena and soon he had her reins on and they were sharing a leisurely walk around the ring. He noticed the cones that had been placed evenly apart and in a straight line.

He smiled and turned Christmas toward the course. He took her through at a walk and felt that she believed it was boring to go at such a slow pace. He turned her around and this time went through at a canter. She completed the course flawlessly and seemed as if she was up to any challenge.

He took her to the opposite side of the arena and off they went to test the jumps. She cleared them with ease, spun around without coaxing and took the jumps in the opposite direction.

When she came to a stop, Jackson threw his head back and laughed. "Sweetheart, under any other circumstance that would've earned you the title of 'Hot Dog' or 'showoff', but not from me. I don't know or care what anybody would say or think, that was one magnificent display of intelligence. I wouldn't care if I was in horse show and you performed that same stunt and we were disqualified, I'd still be happy and very proud of you."

He slid off her back and they walked back to the barn where he rewarded her with two carrots and an apple. Then came a well-deserved brushing and combing, while she relaxed and enjoyed it.

"Well, sweetheart, Christmas is only a matter of days away.

Don't know if I can find mom by then or not. It's sure been a test of my patience tryin' to find her. But I won't give up."

He gently stroked her forelock with a soft brush. "Tonight's the battle of the chefs. Taylor and I are gonna duel over who's the better cook. Although, I don't think it's really much of a battle if you don't prepare the entire meal. It'll be fun anyway. Of course, I can have a good time with Taylor no matter what we're doing."

***

Taylor was busy in the kitchen, working to prove she was a good cook. In spite of her business and its time constraints on her hours in the kitchen, she continued to dazzle family and friends with her culinary skills. As a very young girl she spent many hours in the kitchen with Juanita and learned from a chef she considered one of the very best.

No one knew anything regarding Jackson's cooking skills, but everyone was anxious to taste the steaks he was preparing. He'd taken time to light the fire and make sure it was burning hot and fast so there would be ample mesquite embers. Those hot embers would touch off the additional mesquite when it was added to the fireplace.

Steve and Rose sat on the sofa sipping a Macallan Scotch and talking while they watched Jackson place the steaks on the fireplace grill. Juanita sat in the kitchen talking with Taylor as they sipped a glass of very fine Cabernet.

At last the dinner hour arrived and everyone took their seats at the dining room table. Rose offered the blessing, while everyone bowed their heads and prayed with her.

When the blessing ended, Jackson carried a tray to the table and sat plates with individually labeled steaks in front of each of them, beginning with Rose.

While he was passing out the steaks, Taylor was placing a small plate with the twice-baked potato. Next, she served up a helping of her sautéed mushrooms and, when finished, sat down at the table.

Taylor looked at the flashy red and white label, which had been carefully placed in the center of her steak. The neatly block printed message, in white ink, of "Second Best Chef" immediately caught her attention.

She held it up and looked at Jackson saying, "I must have the wrong steak. Obviously, I have yours."

He smiled. "Oh, no. You have the right steak." He held up his label, which clearly stated, "World's Best Chef."

After a moment of laughter, everyone turned their attention to the food in front of them. All went immediately for their steak, except Jackson who wanted to taste the mushrooms and potato.

"Taylor, you did a fantastic job with the mushrooms and potato," he said. "Best I've ever tasted."

She carefully cut a small portion of steak and soon said, "You really are a good cook. This steak is out of this world."

Soon, Steve, Rose and Juanita were singing his praises for a most sensational tasting Rib Eye steak. By the time everyone had sampled a portion of the entire meal, there was an overall vote of complete satisfaction with dinner.

When the meal ended the vote for best chef ended in a tie and Taylor quickly challenged Jackson to a rematch, which he graciously accepted.

Rose tapped her water glass with a spoon. "Let's not forget, the dance is tomorrow evening at St. Martin's."

Taylor looked at Jackson. "And you hafta wear a suit and tie, not your barn clothes."

"Don't' worry, I have some new jeans, a wrangler jacket and an old shoe lace I can use for a tie."

Rose laughed and said, "Jackson, do you dance?"

He glanced at Taylor for a second and then said, "Oh, I dance a little."

"Well, whether you dance or not, I'm sure you'll have a good time."

"Yes, ma'am, I'm sure I will… as long as Taylor doesn't step on my toes or kick me in the shins."

"You're Taylor's date?" she said with a smile.

"Yes, ma'am. Taylor said all the other available bachelors turned her down and she came to me in desperation and begged me to be her date."

Taylor threw her napkin at him. "I never begged you. I can always stay home and you can go by yourself."

He smiled. "Diane might still be available."

"No, she's not. She already has a date."

"Oh, well," he said. "I guess we're stuck with each other."

"Okay. So, we'll just pretend we like each other and try to have a good time."

"That sounds good. With a little effort, I'm sure we can struggle through the evening without biting or kicking each other."

He stood up and said it was time to make his nightly visit to the barn to bid everyone goodnight and pass out a last treat to all.

Taylor began helping Juanita clear the table while her parents sat at the table and nursed their after-dinner drinks.

Taylor and Juanita said very little as they worked and soon the table was almost cleared.

Taylor had just picked up her empty wine glass when Juanita said, "Pardon me for asking, but Miss Taylor are you in love with Mr. Jackson?"

She dropped her wine glass, but managed to catch it before it fell to the floor. "Uh… Uh… Well, no. I mean… We're just good friends."

"Oh, I'm sorry for asking," she said, noticing Rose nodding her head and smiling. "Well, sometimes good friends can become much more."

"I'll get the dessert plates," Taylor said, ignoring Juanita's last comment.

When Taylor went to the kitchen, Rose said to Steve, "I wish they'd hurry up and stop all this pretending. I can't take much more of this waiting for them to make up their minds."

"Now, Rose, settle down. It's not the mind that'll take care of their problem, it's their hearts. And you should know that better than anyone."

"I just hope he won't hafta lock her in a closet to get her to admit she loves him."

"Rose, I wouldn't worry about it. He'll probably just toss her backside in the horse trough again."

Seventeen

Saturday morning the sun came peeking up over the treetops and its brilliant golden rays told of a beautiful day ahead. The snow on the ground glistened and the fluffy powder sparkled in the trees, and along fence railings.

Birds swooped in and sat on the edges of the half dozen bird feeders that Rose had put up in various locations around the house. Of course, about a dozen crows wanted to stake a claim to the entire cache of birdseed, though the Cardinals and other assorted birds took exception and sent them packing—at least temporarily.

Jackson returned from the barn after the morning feeding and found Steve waiting in the kitchen for him.

"Jackson could you do me a favor?"

"Yes, sir."

"Taylor has to pick up her car from the dealership sometime before noon. Unfortunately, I have a business appointment and I was wondering if you could take her."

"No problem at all, Whitfield."

"Thank you."

When Jackson left the room, Rose noticed the big grin on her husband's face.

"Okay, Steven, what've you done this time?"

"Nothing, dear, I just asked Jackson to take Taylor to pick up her car."

"Well, I can't believe it took this long to repair her car."

He tried to hide his smile, but it was no use and Rose knew for certain he'd pulled off another of his schemes... a scheme to keep putting Taylor and Jackson together.

"Steven, that's it," she said, tossing a towel on the counter. "I wanna know what little stunt you've cooked up."

"Uh... Well, Taylor's car was actually totaled. I just forgot to tell her and ..."

"Oh, no, Steven Whitfield, you didn't forget. You just found a convenient way to keep Taylor and Jackson together."

"Now, Rose, there's no need to get upset about it. I think she and Jackson are gonna work things out. Besides, Taylor didn't really need a car when..."

"When she had Jackson Riley's Taxi Service, compliments of you. Steven, you know Taylor needs a car."

"I've already picked a new car for her. It'll be ready when she and Jackson get there."

"You bought her a new car?"

He lowered his head. "Yeah. I guess after my rather devious plan, it was the least I could do."

"Steven, some of the things you've done in the past surprised me. But I came to understand that it was just the way you are. But I never believed I'd see the day when you went above and beyond to push your daughter into the arms of a man. Most father's never see any man as good enough for their daughters, but you seem so much at ease when she's with Jackson."

"So, you object to the idea of her being with Jackson?"

"Oh, no, not at all. I think they're an ideal couple."

He shook his head. "You just couldn't wait to unload that one on me."

"You deserved it."

About thirty-minutes later they watched Jackson and Taylor walk out to his truck. He opened the door for her and bowed as he stepped back to allow her to pass and get in the truck. She obviously said something to him, and they assumed it had to be some type of smart retort.

They stopped for breakfast at the Cedar Falls Diner before driving to the car dealership. With Barb being off this Saturday, breakfast was very dull due to a lack of the usual entertaining battle of wits. But they managed to suffer through the boredom.

By 10:30 AM they were walking into the service department door at Carson's BMW. The service manager quickly directed her to the front office where Walt Carson greeted her.

She seemed stunned when he began telling her that her car had been so severely damaged it couldn't be repaired. Taylor was shaking her head when he told her that a brand-new Sapphire Black Metallic, 430i Coupe had been purchased, and paid in full and was prepped and ready to go. She needed only to sign the necessary papers and she would be on her way.

Moments later she stared blankly at the car while Jackson gave it the once, twice and three times over.

"Now, that's a car," he said, smiling. "Black leather interior and a cockpit to rival the Starship Enterprise. Man, this sweet ride's gonna turn some heads."

Walt Carson gave her the grand guided tour of her new car and pointed out all the latest accessories. When her tutorial ended, he gave her the keys and wished her the best.

Jackson followed her home and stood back and smiled while she tearfully hugged her father. She was stammering to find the right words of thanks, but for the time being a simple "Thank you" was all she could muster.

Time on this Saturday was not standing still. The dinner hour was moved to four o'clock and it was decided they would all attend

Mass together before the dance.

Barn chores had been taken over by Jose and George, but it was a safe bet that Jackson would at least stop by and see Christmas. And, sure enough, he stopped by long enough to give her a kiss and a few carrots before heading back to the house to shower and dress for the dance.

Taylor walked down the stairs from her room and her mother immediately approved of her attire. She wore a long, red evening gown, a matching jacket with gold buttons, red high-heeled shoes and a string of pearls. Her blonde hair fell just below her shoulders and, as always for dressy occasions, not a hair out of place.

She was talking with her parents when Jackson walked into the living room.

She turned her head and whispered, "Wow!"

He wore a charcoal gray suit, which had been altered to fit his physique. With the suit, he was wearing a red shirt and, for the Christmas Season, a black tie adorned with green holly leaves and red berries. On his lapel he had placed a pin of The American Flag and Marine Corps Emblem.

He walked directly to Taylor and completely surprised her with a corsage. Without hesitation he pinned it perfectly to her jacket, stepped back and smiled.

She looked into his eyes and said, "You absolutely amaze me. I didn't expect this and you didn't hafta do it."

"Oh, I disagree. A beautiful woman should have a beautiful flower."

Steve said, "Well, are we ready to go?"

"Jackson and I can take my car," Taylor said. With that she turned and handed the keys to Jackson. "Please, you drive."

He took the keys. "You're really gonna trust me with your new car?"

She smiled. "I didn't say I trusted you."

Jackson laughed. "Well, I walked right into that. Seems I've heard it somewhere before."

"And, I'll be grading your driving and your ability to handle the car."

He shook his head. "This could be a long night. I didn't know I'd hafta take a driving test."

They arrived at St. Martin's and were greeted at the door by a group of ushers. After a few handshakes and greetings, they turned to enter the main church when Robby and Samantha Swanson called out to Jackson and ran over to him.

He dropped to one knee and happily accepted a hug from each and a kiss on the cheek from Samantha. A moment or two of idle chatter and they hurried back to their grandfather who gave a nod of recognition to Jackson.

While walking to their pew, Jackson was acknowledged with a number of smiles, a few handshakes and some words of thanks and praise.

Father Kurt, a stickler for punctuality, stood at the back of the church and signaled the organist that it was time to begin. As always, he wasted little time, and his homily was direct and on point for the Christmas Season and over in five-minutes. It wasn't at all surprising when the Mass ended ten-minutes early.

Many exiting the church were also going to the Christmas dance and there was a steady stream of parishioners walking to the church hall. Coat checking and table assignments took up several minutes, but at last everyone was seated at their respective tables.

Diane Wilson and her date, along with Walt and Beverly Carson and Bart and Michele Jennings joined them at their table.

In no time at all, Sheriff Jennings had Jackson pulled to the side and it was obvious they were involved in a serious discussion. Finally, the sheriff smiled, shook Jackson's hand and they returned to the table.

Steve glanced across the table and said, "Well, Bart, you seem rather happy. What's up?"

"I have the okay for this, so let me introduce you to Deputy Sheriff Jackson Riley."

Questions and comments came from almost everyone at the same time. Jackson and Sheriff Jennings took turns answering the queries and acknowledging congratulations.

When the clamor settled, the music began and, as Taylor had said, the first number of the evening was for those who dared step to the floor for Ballroom Dancing.

Rose looked at Steve who tried to pretend he didn't see the hint she was sending. But suddenly she glanced up when Jackson took her by the arm and she appeared very surprised by his action.

Taylor was smiling when Jackson took her mother by the arm and led her to the dance floor. She knew his secret, but was anxious to see how well he could really dance.

"You know how to Ballroom Dance?" Rose said.

"Oh, yes, ma'am. One of those fringe benefits of going to military school, but when being forced to participate it wasn't that much fun. But now I'm glad I was made to take part in the dance classes."

Jackson and Rose were the only couple on the dance floor and, much to everyone's surprise, they were moving around the floor as though they had danced together for years.

No one else took to the dance floor while Jackson and Rose moved about in near perfect harmony. As the song drew to an end, they were toasted with a very boisterous ovation.

Rose tightly held Jackson's arm as they exited the floor and walked to their table. There they were greeted with another round of applause. Though it was the smile on Steve's face that clearly said, if Rose still harbored any doubts about Jackson, they were dispelled on the dance floor.

Diane looked at Jackson and said, "Well, you certainly are full of surprises. Where did you learn to dance like that?"

"Oh, just one of those things I picked up as a kid."

Of course, Jackson wasn't at all prepared for the onslaught of women who suddenly wanted to dance with him. And, leading the charge was Casey Swanson, Bob Swanson's youngest daughter.

For the next hour, he was unable to make it back to the table to sit down. Although it was Casey Swanson who seemed to want his complete and undivided attention. She whisked him away at every opportunity and dragged him back to the dance floor.

Finally, he raised his hands and said it was time for a break. He made it back to the table and sat down, took a deep breath and eagerly accepted the cold glass of beer Steve offered.

Taylor smiled, leaned close and said, "You certainly left a lotta women panting."

He shook his head. "Yeah, and Casey Swanson needs a muzzle."

"Well, it sure looked like she was trying her best to talk you to death."

He took a sip of beer. "Oh, she was tryin' her best, but it wasn't sweet nothings she was whispering in my ear."

"You mean she was…"

"I have a question for you, Riley," Ward Swanson, the oldest Swanson son said, cutting her off.

Jackson eased his chair back, stood up and looked across the table at him. "What is it?"

"You've grabbed quite a bit of publicity since you rolled into town. Personally, I don't know why. Just what've you done that I haven't?"

Jackson slowly walked around the table until he was standing face to face with Ward Swanson. "I've walked through the fires of hell, looked straight into the eyes of death and spit in the face of the devil."

Swanson backed up a step, turned and walked away without uttering a word.

Jackson returned to his chair, sat down, looked at Taylor and said, "Where were we?"

"Uh... I... You really put Ward in his place."

"Hey, he said he wanted to ask me a question. If he doesn't wanna hear the truth, he shouldn't ask the question."

Steve nodded. "That was some response. I have no doubt every word of it was true and I'll leave it at that."

"Thank you, sir."

The lights grew a little dimmer and there was another rush of women asking Jackson to dance.

He politely declined, saying, "I promised Taylor she could have every dance for the rest of the evening."

Taylor took his hand. "Okay. Then you can start now."

They made their way to the dance floor and found a spot in the center. Without hesitation Jackson took Taylor in his arms and she put her arms around him. They looked into each other's eyes and two hearts were off and racing.

Taylor swallowed and half whispered, "I... I think I should warn you."

"Warn me?"

"I rubbed the back of my gown with poison ivy," she said, hoping she could lighten the mood and keep what she really wanted under control.

He laughed. "I guess if I hafta catch it, I couldn't think of a more pleasant way."

He provided another opening for her to keep the mood light. "Oh, really? I thought you said you'd rather hug poison ivy than put your arms around me."

"Maybe I lied."

"Just like you lied about not training your horse to push me into your arms."

Now it was his turn. "So, what if I did train her to do that?"

"Well... Well... That makes you guilty of... uh... guilty of something."

"Guilty of wanting my arms around you?" he said, holding her just a little tighter.

"Yes," she blurted.

"What does that make you guilty of?"

She didn't say a word. She placed her cheek against his and hugged tighter thinking, *I can't go on like this much longer. I'm half out of my mind, wanting to throw my arms around him and tell him I'm in love with him.*

When the music stopped, they walked hand in hand to their table. They were in the process of sitting down when someone took Jackson by the arm.

"You're not gettin' outta here without at least one dance with me." It was Barb.

He smiled. "My pleasure. Besides, this should make up for not seein' you at the diner this morning."

As soon as they began to dance she let him have it. "Okay, Jackson, don't you dare lie to me."

"What?"

"Don't you dare tell me that you're not in love with Taylor."

He shook his head. "As long as you won't repeat it, yes, I'm in love with Taylor. I'd like to keep that quiet just a little longer."

"I'll keep it a secret on one condition."

"What's that?"

"I expect an invitation to the wedding."

"Oh, hey, we're just movin' right along here. You already have us at the Altar."

She laughed. "Trust me, that's exactly where you're headed."

"I won't argue with you."

The dance drew to a close and the hall slowly emptied as everyone continued to talk while exiting the building. Of course, after being inside the six degree temperature was a quite a shock. Once outside, everybody hurried at a brisk pace to their cars in search of shelter from the bitter cold.

Taylor seemed happy on the drive home and sang along with the Christmas Carols. She tried to get Jackson to sing with her, but he declined, saying he didn't want to embarrass her. Then confessed that he'd be much more comfortable howling along with a pack of wolves.

Once home, Taylor went to her room, but Jackson did a quick change and went to the barn to see Christmas.

He opened the stall door and as she began walking out, he said, "Christmas, I almost blew it tonight. I had Taylor in my arms on the dance floor and temptation was workin' overtime tryin' to get me to tell her how I feel about her."

She turned her head just a little and, once again, there was a gleam in her eyes that he was certain said she understood exactly what he was saying.

He kissed her on the nose. "Well, at least I can tell you I love you." He put his hands on the sides of her face and kissed her again. "Goodnight, my beautiful girl."

Eighteen

As always, Jackson was up early on Sunday morning and at the barn feeding the horses, dogs and cats before the sun even began its ascent in the eastern sky.

When he was finished, he went to the diner alone, knowing all in the Whitfield household planned on sleeping in today. Barb greeted him, but was disappointed that Taylor hadn't accompanied him. She laughed when Jackson told her she'd just have to fill in for her.

After breakfast he returned to the farm and went directly to his room. He turned on the computer and sat down with his coffee Barb had given him on his way out the door.

He opened the search engine and began again looking for Mary Barton. He was trying to tell himself to be prepared for one more day of disappointment when an image appeared on the screen.

He grabbed his wallet and pulled out the faded photograph. A moment later his heart pace picked up. The woman's face on the computer screen bore a very striking resemblance to his mother.

He looked closer, carefully studying her features, and after a few long minutes he was certain he'd found her. He checked into her background and learned that she was listed as the Executive

Assistant to the head of a major law firm in South Carolina. In her personal bio he found that she was originally from River's Edge. That piece of information was enough to convince him beyond doubt that he'd found his mother.

He immediately packed a bag and went online to book a flight to Charleston, South Carolina. The earliest flight he could take was 4:00 PM, so he'd have plenty of time to talk with Mr. Whitfield and spend some time with Christmas.

Steve Whitfield was walking down the stairs when he saw Jackson pacing in the living room.

"Anything wrong?"

"Sir, I need to talk with you. It's very important."

"Why don't we talk over a late breakfast?"

"Yes, sir. That's fine."

Barb caught a glimpse of them walking toward the door and picked up two menus. As soon as they entered the diner, she escorted them to a booth at the back of the diner.

She handed them a menu and said, "Be right back with coffee and orange juice. She looked at Jackson. "And, I'm guessing you're here to eat again because the first time wasn't enough."

He nodded. "Yeah, gotta take care of the bottomless pit."

When she walked away Steve said, "What's on your mind, Jackson?"

"Mr. Whitfield, I've found my mother. She's living in South Carolina."

He was quiet for a moment and then said, "When do you wanna leave?"

"I've booked a flight for four o'clock this afternoon."

He nodded. "Good. Do you want me to drive you to the airport?"

"No, sir. I appreciate the offer, but I can park my truck and leave it there. I don't wanna inconvenience you."

"Son, you won't be inconveniencing me."

Jackson shook his head. "Sir, I'm already leavin' you with little notice and someone's gonna hafta pick up my barn duties."

Steve smiled. "Well, like you, I'm not allergic to hard work. I can pick up the slack for a few mornings and I'm sure I can talk Jose and George into takin' care of the evening feeding and stalling."

"I still hate leavin' you…"

Steve raised a hand. "Jackson, it's more important for you to go see your mother. I'm sure there's a lotta things you two need to catch up on."

"Well, sir, I don't mind tellin' you I'm really nervous about this."

"I can imagine you would be. How old were you the last time you saw or spoke with your mother?"

He thought for a moment and said, "I think I was ten-years old."

"So it's been what, seventeen or eighteen years?"

"Gettin' close to eighteen years now."

"That's a long time."

He took a deep breath. "Yes, sir. I just hope we can put our lives back together. I'd sure like havin' her back in my life."

"I'll say a prayer that everything works out for you."

"Thank you, Mr. Whitfield. I'm sure a few prayers would be very helpful."

"Do you still want this kept between us?"

"Yes, sir. I'd rather wait 'til I see how things work out before I say anything to Taylor or Mrs. Whitfield."

"It'll stay between us."

"Thank you. And I hope to be back by Wednesday."

"Okay, and when you get a little time call and let me know how things are going."

"Yes, sir."

***

After returning to Whitfield Acres, Jackson quietly slipped in the back door, changed clothes and went to the barn. He brought Christmas in from the pasture, removed her blanket and started to brush her forelock.

"Sweetheart, I've gotta leave for a few days, but don't worry, I'll never abandon you. You're my savior when things feel bad. I know I can always come to you and tell you what's on my mind. It's easy talkin' with you and you never seem to care about my rambling on sometimes when I have a lot on my mind.

"I found my mom after a long search and I hafta go see her and hope we can put our lives back together. It was tough bein' a kid and losin' my mother because of a pack of lies. And then a judge tells her she can't see me again because she's an unfit mother. She wasn't. She was a good mother who tried her best to make my life a happy one, but dad's constant drinkin' and abuse just tore us apart as a family.

"I feel guilty because I didn't start tryin' to find her sooner, but I guess earlier wasn't the right time. I sure hope and pray that this is the right time."

He groomed her for over an hour, gave her a few carrots and some spiced apple treats before returning her to the pasture. He gave her a kiss on the nose and gently ran his hand up and down her face. He kissed her once more and said, "I'm sure gonna miss you, girl."

He returned to the house and went out of his way to avoid Taylor and Mrs. Whitfield. He wasn't ready to try and explain what he was doing. He showered, changed clothes and quietly exited via the back door.

He put the suitcase on the floor on the passenger's side of the truck and headed for the airport. The drive took almost forty-five minutes and he was surprised how easily he found a parking space. He breezed through check in and had time for a quick sandwich before boarding.

He tried to nap during the flight, but thoughts of what might be ahead kept him awake. Of course, that made the flight seem as though it would never end. It felt more like he was flying to Japan rather than South Carolina.

At last the plane touched down and within the hour he was checked in to his hotel. The hotel dining room offered an excellent selection from sandwiches to steak and lobster and roasted chicken. He opted for roasted chicken with baked potato and green beans, and a chocolate mousse for dessert.

He returned to his room and looked up the law firm of Davis, Greenberg and Johnson. He was happy to find that they were located only a few blocks away and probably no more then a fifteen-minute walk.

Jackson had a restless night, tossing and turning as his mind raced through every conceivable scenario for seeing his mother for the first time in almost eighteen years. Would she recognize him? How would she react to seeing him? Did she still love him? These thoughts and more played over and over, pulling him from his sleep and adding to his anticipation.

He was up by five-thirty, showering and dressing. He went to the hotel dining room around six-thirty, but realized his normal ravenous appetite was almost non-existent. He sipped a coffee and managed to eat a blueberry muffin while constantly glancing at his watch.

Time now was in slow motion and he was beginning to ask himself if the 9:00 AM opening time for the law firm would ever arrive. He drank a second cup of coffee and returned to his room.

He tried to occupy himself by watching the news, although he didn't hear a word the commentators said. He switched to the sports channel and then to a rerun of NCIS, which held his attention until eight o'clock.

He switched off the TV, picked up a lightweight jacket and left his room. He skipped the elevator and took the stairs down from the tenth floor, hoping the walk would eat away at the time. But lady luck didn't cooperate.

He began walking as his mind again took off in a swirling mass of "what ifs." At one point he suddenly stopped, looked at his reflection in a store window and forced a smile. There would be no answers until he at last met face to face with his mother. With that in mind, he took a deep breath and continued on his way.

He arrived at the office building, checked the lobby directory and found the office of Davis, Greenberg and Johnson was located on the fifth floor. He'd walk up in lieu of the elevator ride and hoped a few more minutes would tick off his watch.

He walked into the hallway, turned left and found he was only a few steps from the doorway of the law firm. He hesitated, trying to compose his thoughts before entering.

At last he opened the door and walked to the receptionist's desk. When she looked up he said, "Good morning. I'd like to see Mary Barton if she's in."

The young lady smiled. "She's not in yet, but she should be here any minute. Can you tell me what this is in reference to?"

"Uh... It's a long story and would take..."

"Oh, there she is now," she said, looking toward the door.

Jackson turned slowly as his heart began to race. Walking toward him was a very attractive, impeccably dressed woman who he knew in an instant was his mother. He took a few steps in her direction and stopped.

The last time he saw her she was 29 years old, yet somehow she looked younger now. Perhaps it was the strain of those years of abuse and hardship being lifted from her shoulders that made her look so youthful.

Suddenly, she stopped and stared at him. She dropped her briefcase and stammered. "Oh... Oh, my God! Jackson!" She raised her hand to her mouth, shook her head and began sobbing.

He was struggling to hold himself together as he hurried to her and wrapped his arms around her. She buried her face against his shoulder and held tightly to the son she'd thought was gone forever from her life.

He swallowed hard and held her as tears trickled down his face. All of a sudden a lifetime of pain and doubt was gone. He'd found what he'd lost so many years ago and the heartache seemed as though it had never really been there.

At last she took a step back and looked into her son's eyes. "It's really you. I... I've... I've prayed for this day," she said as he began wiping away her tears. "But... I... I wasn't sure my prayers... would be answered."

He nodded. "I... I've missed you. And... and I wasn't sure I'd ever see you again."

She took his handkerchief and wiped at her eyes. "I... I can hardly believe it's really you." She smiled through the tears. "And just look at you. You... You're so handsome and goodness you look so strong. I..." She began crying again.

"Mary, is everything okay?"

She glanced over at Myron Davis. "Oh, please, you... you'll hafta excuse me. This is a very emotional moment for me. But, yes everything is fine now, Mr. Davis." She took a deep breath. "This is my son, Jackson Riley."

Suddenly a rapid string of congratulations, introductions and explanations were circulating through the quickly growing crowd in the lobby.

Senior partners Paul Greenberg and Darrin Johnson joined the group and when the impromptu celebration settled down they spoke with Myron Davis and all agreed Mary needed the day to reconnect with her son.

Davis approached her and said, "Mary, we want you to take the day off to be with your son. But, you know we'll need you here tomorrow and at least a few hours on Wednesday so we can finalize the Baxter and Masters merger contract."

"Thank you so much," she said, wiping at her eyes again. "I can't tell you how happy I am at this moment and I doubt that I'd be much help to you today anyway."

He smiled. "That's quite understandable."

She turned to Jackson. "Would you like to have breakfast?"

He grinned. "Absolutely. At the moment I'm ready to eat a steer and have a another for dessert."

"We have three great restaurants right here in the building. So, we won't hafta go far."

He kissed her on the cheek, took her by the arm and left the office. In a matter of a few minutes they were seated at a table with a coffee and waiting to have their breakfast order taken.

She shook her head and looked across the table at Jackson. "I don't even know where to begin. There's so much I want to know and right now, my mind is so jumbled with questions I'm lost."

"Me too, mom. So, don't worry."

"I feel so bad that I lost touch with you," she said, fighting to hold back the tears. "But everything became a nightmare when Bill and Susan had you taken from me." She paused and fought to keep her composure. "Then all of those lies they told in court and their friends supported their statements."

"Mom, believe me, I know nothing was your fault. I know they lied." He shook his head. "They shipped me off to a military school and lied to me about so much when I asked about you. I tried to send letters to you, but it was obvious after a while that the letters weren't being mailed by school officials. When I was finally able to get to a telephone, I tried to call but was told the number had been disconnected."

"Jackson, I just had to get out of River's Edge," she said as she struggled to keep her composure. "After the hearing so many people turned on me and actually believed everything was my fault."

"Mom, right now, the only thing that matters to me is that I found you." He smiled. "I have so much to tell you and especially about a very exceptional woman."

Suddenly she took on a new glow. "Oh, my. Am I close to

having a daughter-in-law in my future?"

Now it was his turn to glow. "Mom, I fell in love with her the day we met. And, believe me, our first meeting was definitely unique."

"I can't wait to hear the whole story."

They ate breakfast and sat at the table and talked until almost noon. The waitress didn't mind because she was well aware that the law firm would be picking up the tab and there was always a very generous gratuity included.

***

Back at Whitfield Acres, Taylor was in a gloomy mood as she walked into the barn late Monday evening. She walked down the aisle and stopped at Christmas's stall.

She looked at her and said, "I know you miss him as much as I do. I can't believe how empty I feel without him. I mean it. Not having him around feels so strange and I haven't even known him that long."

She passed a spiced apple treat to Christmas. "But, I sure have known him long enough to fall head over heels in love with him. I know it might sound crazy, but I think I actually fell in love with him when he threw me in the horse trough. "

Christmas nodded her head up and down three times and gave a little nicker.

"Are you laughing at me?" she said, looking at the beautiful mare. "I swear you are. You're laughing about Jackson throwing me in the trough."

Taylor smiled and handed her another treat. "I wish I knew what was so important that he had to leave town without saying a word to me. And, Dad won't tell me. He says he's sure Jackson's gonna explain everything when he gets back. I sure hope it's soon. When he gets back, I'm just gonna tell him how I feel. I can't go on like this any longer. If I'm in his arms one more time and he doesn't kiss me, I swear I'm gonna kick him in the shins."

She kissed Christmas on the nose. "That's from Jackson."

She walked to Bronson's stall and gave him an apple treat. "I know I'm not my normal smiling self this evening. I'm sorry. I guess I'm gonna be walking around with this dark cloud over my head feeling until Jackson gets back.

"Sometimes I think my feelings for Jackson are just plain crazy. But then I must admit that I've never had the feelings for another man that I have for Jackson. So, there I was wasting time looking for Mr. Perfect Dream Lover and along comes somebody completely different. I snap orders to him and he just smiles and, in his own polite way, tells me he'll listen when he's ready. I bark at him again and 'splash' there I am in the water trough. And before I know it, he's making my heart pound, my knees weak and I have all these butterflies fluttering in my stomach."

She passed another treat to Bronson and gently scratched him under the chin. "Oh, Bronson, what am I gonna do? I don't know." She took a deep breath. "When he gets back maybe I should just walk up to him, grab him and kiss him until he screams to come up for air. Then, I'll tell him I love him and I'm gonna marry him and kiss him again. That should seal our relationship permanently."

She stepped back, gave Bronson one last treat and returned to the house. A few minutes later she was looking at her image in the mirror and smiling.

That's it. I've made up my mind. Jackson when you get home, I'm not even gonna give you a chance to say hello. I'm just gonna throw my arms around you and kiss you. I know it's what I want. I know it's what you want and that's it. We're both gonna find our dream come true.

She turned off the light, got into bed and smiled once again. "Jackson, you were right," she whispered. "I do feel so much better after talking with Bronson and Christmas. And, I told them both a secret. Now they know I love you."

***

Jackson spent the better part of Tuesday playing phone tag with Steve. He informed Steve that his mother would be coming to Cedar Falls for Christmas and staying at the Cedar Falls Inn. Steve's return message said there was more than enough room for her at the house and she could stay there.

It was early evening when they finally connected. Jackson thanked him for his offer and said he was sure his mother would accept the invitation.

"Mr. Whitfield, we do have a major conflict though. Mom can't fly in until Christmas Eve morning. Her flight gets in at ten, but I'm already committed to pickin' up Gunny Davidson and takin' him to the hotel to meet his family. Now, Sheriff Jennings called and asked me to help out at a big Santa Claus surprise event that Mayor Bostwick's hosting for needy children and their families. That's at 10:00 AM. I..."

"Jackson, don't worry about a thing. Rose and I can pick up your mother and bring her back to the house."

"I certainly appreciate that, Mr. Whitfield, but I don't wanna impose on you, especially on Christmas Eve."

"Nonsense. It won't be a problem." He laughed. "Besides, all my shopping's done and I know Rose had her shopping done by Thanksgiving."

"Thank you. And, when I get back I'm gonna ask Taylor if she can help out with the Santa event."

"Good idea. I'm sure she'll be happy to help."

"My return flight's scheduled to get in around eight o'clock Wednesday evening."

"Rose and I won't be home Wednesday evening. So, give me a call when you arrive at the house and let me know if there's any change in plans for Christmas Eve."

"Yes, sir, I'll do that. And thanks again."

***

Jackson and his mother once again sat down and talked after

dinner, trying to fill in the blanks from their years apart. At times, it was emotional for both, but a blessing to know that in their hearts their love for each other never faltered.

She learned of Jackson's time in the military school, his days as a college student and his six years of service to America in the Marine Corps. Yet, he would not share any details of those months spent in foreign lands and the missions.

Naturally, his mother kept returning to his relationship with Taylor and was very happy to know he was preparing to take a much bigger step with this young lady. She was anxious to meet her and see for herself what made her so special to her son. He showed her dozens of photos of Taylor and swore none of them could show how beautiful she really was. In so many of the pictures it was evident she wasn't posing for the camera and those were the ones Jackson had taken when she was unaware and just herself.

Of course, she was also anxious to meet the Whitfield family and get to know them. They too seemed to mean a great deal to her son and she was grateful that they accepted him as if he was a family member. He spoke highly of them and she gathered rather quickly that he was a good judge of character.

She was also eager to meet this very wonderful horse called Christmas that was so much a part of his life. The pictures of her appeared to show a very loving, magnificent horse and somehow she could tell, even from a photo, the love she had for her son. And, she knew there was a very unique bond between Jackson and Christmas. She wondered if they were each other's saviors.

Jackson found that his mother picked up the pieces of what was left of her life in River's Edge and moved away. Her life there had been ruined by lies and innuendo and, rather than suffer through the torment, she moved on. In time the physical scars healed and melted away, but the mental anguish had to be dealt with by many long months of counseling. Yet, thus far, she had been unable to regain the trust she needed to establish a trusting relationship with another man.

She went on to college and eventually went to work as a paralegal and became a very trusted assistant to Myron Davis. She was very happy with her position in the firm and their confidence and trust in her abilities gave her a terrific boost in her self-esteem.

Reluctantly, they ended their conversation shortly after nine. They would have only a little time together on Wednesday, but there was so much to look forward to in the days ahead.

Nineteen

Jackson met his mother for a very early breakfast, being the first patrons of the day when the restaurant opened its doors. They would have almost three hours together before she had to be at work and they tried to make the most of it.

"Jackson, you've told me so much about Taylor, but not how you met her."

He laughed. "Well, mom, our first meeting was, shall we say, very interesting and most unusual."

"Really?"

"Oh, yes."

She reached for her coffee cup. "Now, you've really got me curious. What happened?"

Again, he laughed. "Well, I was workin' in the barn, in the tack room actually, when she came in and without so much as a 'hi, how are you?' she snaps an order at me to saddle her horse. Well, after a few verbal exchanges and a battle of wills, I picked her up and threw her in a horse trough."

"No! You didn't!"

"Yes, I did."

"And, you still fell in love with her."

He shrugged. "Mom, I think it was inevitable. Actually, I truly believe I fell in love with her that day."

"Well, it certainly is a most unusual introduction."

He smiled. "Then we engaged in some verbal dueling after that, laced with a number of threats and veiled promises."

"Why did the two of you continue seeing each other, if that's the right choice of words?"

"Mr. Whitfield seemed to keep finding ways or excuses to put us together. At first, I wasn't sure why he was doing it, but later I began to suspect that he was purposely looking for ways to keep us together. What really threw me a curve was his insisting that Taylor and I pick out the family Christmas tree."

She smiled. "Now, I can't wait to meet Mr. Whitfield. He must be one fine judge of character if he chose to find ways to keep the two of you together. And wanting the two of you to pick out the family Christmas tree tells me he's expecting something permanent to develop between you and Taylor."

"I kinda suspected that too."

"How did the Christmas tree search go?"

He laughed and said, "Well, mom, that was an adventure that would've been comedy material if somebody had filmed it."

He related the tale of the Great Christmas Tree Caper, as he now called it, to his mother and made certain he didn't omit any of the intimate details.

His mother began laughing heartily as the story progressed but when he reached the part where Taylor pulled the mask over his eyes, she couldn't hold back any longer. At this point her laughter could best be described as very enthusiastic. But, when he told her of Taylor toppling backward into the pile of snow and his ending up on top of her, it was definitely time for a restroom break.

It took a few minutes for her to regain her composure and then she had to reapply her makeup before rejoining Jackson at the table.

The waitress took their orders and suddenly it seemed their time together was ending much too quickly. Yet, it wouldn't be long before they'd spend a real Christmas together.

***

Jackson arrived at Whitfield Acres by early evening. When he noticed that Taylor's car wasn't there, he changed clothes and went to the barn.

Christmas began shuffling around in her stall the moment she heard his voice. By the time he reached the gate it looked as though she was dancing with delight. He gave her a quick kiss on the nose and offered her a peppermint treat. She accepted it, but only after another kiss on the nose.

He brought her out and began grooming her while telling the story of his trip to meet his mother. "Christmas, finding my mom after all these years and finally seeing her again was unbelievable. I can't tell you how happy I was being able to put my arms around her and hug her.

"Being able to spend time with her took so much off my mind. Now, I can settle down and tell Taylor how I feel about her and hope we can start planning our future."

He gave her another peppermint treat. "Of course, I told mom all about you and she can't wait to meet you. I know you're gonna love her too."

While he went on grooming Christmas and talking with her, Taylor arrived home. The instant she saw Jackson's truck her heart jumped into her throat. Her hands were shaking as she opened the door and got out of her car.

She took a deep breath and thought, *well, Taylor, it's time to look Jackson straight in the eyes and tell him you love him.* She took another deep breath. *I can't hold back any longer and I'm not gonna lose any more sleep over my feelings for him. I still think the best approach is to just throw my arms around him and kiss him. That might be a shock to him, but it sure will be the biggest hint I can give about how I feel.*

She walked briskly to the barn, but very cautiously opened the door. She wanted to take him completely by surprise. His back was to her and he was talking on his phone.

"Yes, sir, it was sheer happiness finding her again after all these years. She was shocked to see me, but after the tears, a hug and a kiss, we started to put things back together. We still have a long way to go to catch up on everything, but at least we're off to a great start." He paused. "Yes, Sir. Her flight's still scheduled to get in at ten tomorrow morning."

Taylor slowly backed out the door, trembling from head to toe. She was having trouble catching her breath and the tears were already burning her eyes. She began half running, half stumbling toward her car. She had to get away from the house, the barn and most of all Jackson.

He... he has a girlfriend. I can't... how did this happen? I... I thought he loved me. I... I was sure he knew I... I loved him. Why didn't... why didn't he tell me? And... and she's coming here. I... I can't believe this is happening.

She managed to start her car and a few moments later she was driving, but had no idea where she was headed. She lost track of time, but shortly after eight o'clock she was knocking on Diane's door.

"Taylor, what's wrong?" she blurted when she opened the door.

"Diane, he... he has a girlfriend," she sobbed.

"Who? Who has a girlfriend?"

"Jackson."

"What! No, no way. He's in love with you."

"Diane, I heard him... he... he was talking on the phone and... and I heard him say they were... they were putting things back together."

She took her hand and led her to the living room. "Taylor,

are you sure that's what you heard?"

"Yes," she sobbed, burying her face in her hands. "I... I... I can't... I can't believe I really fell... fell in love with him and... and now I find out that all... all this time he's... he's had a girlfriend."

Diane poured a glass of wine for her and put a box of tissues on the coffee table. She took her coat, hung it in the closet and sat down beside her.

"Taylor, try and pull yourself together. Think through this again. Try to recall everything and be very certain that Jackson has another woman. I mean I just can't believe it."

She began sobbing uncontrollably and gasped to catch her breath. When she calmed somewhat, she grabbed the glass of wine and gulped it down. She held the glass out to Diane.

"Taylor, I don't believe it's a good idea to guzzle wine and try to think. You need a clear head."

"I... I heard him say she's... she's coming here tomorrow."

"This doesn't make any sense. Why in the world would he bring a girlfriend here? I mean, if he had a girlfriend, which I still find very hard to believe."

"I... I don't know."

"You're absolutely sure you heard him say she was coming here tomorrow?"

"Yes."

"Do you want me to go talk with him?"

She shook her head. "No. Just... Let me... Oh, I... I don't know what to do."

"Well, somehow you've got to pull yourself together. Then we can talk this through and see if we can find out exactly what's going on."

"I can't go home tonight. I just couldn't face him."

"You know you can stay here." She smiled. "You always keep clothes here for night's just like this. I'm sorry. Not like this but..."

Diane, I know what you mean," she said, wiping at her eyes.

Her phone began ringing and she saw Jackson's name on the screen. She declined the call and dropped the phone on the table. He called back immediately and she let it ring until it went to voicemail.

A minute later Diane said, "Aren't you gonna see what the message is?"

"No. I don't care what it is."

"Taylor, you're gonna hafta face him sooner or later and talk with him."

"I'll… I'll do it tomorrow." She lowered her head, reached for a tissue and wiped at her eyes. "And tomorrow's Christmas Eve. Can… Can you believe that? What a… a Christmas this is gonna turn out to be."

Diane took her hand and again tried to console her friend, but it seemed useless. Taylor was crushed and, at this moment, nothing Diane said would help ease her pain.

Taylor's phone began ringing again. Diane picked it up and tapped out a quick text to Jackson.

"Can't talk now. Staying at Diane's tonight. Catch up with you tomorrow."

Jackson read the message twice and shook his head, asking himself what was going on. He looked back at Christmas and said, "This sure is a strange message. I wonder if something's wrong?"

He tried to call Steve, but as had been the case over the past days, his phone went straight to voicemail. He punched in Rose's number, but her phone too went to voicemail.

He thought about calling Diane, but suddenly he felt that he should just wait and talk with Taylor the following day.

"Sweetheart, I sure can't figure out what's goin' on here," he said, as he picked up another brush. "So, I guess I'll just hafta wait 'til tomorrow and find out."

Jackson brushed her for another half-hour before giving her a final treat and sending her to her stall. She closed the gate and he kissed her goodnight.

Before leaving the barn, he passed out treats to Rooster and Rita, Hank, Sylvester and Sylvia. Next, he went from stall to stall and gave a peppermint treat to the horses and ponies. His last stop was Bronson's stall and he received what he guessed was a butt chewing for being absent for a few days.

"Hey, big boy, you don't set the ground rules here. I can't be here everyday just to please you."

Bronson tapped a hoof on the stall floor three times and gave a blunt snort. A second later he snatched the peppermint treat from Jackson's hand and retreated to the back of his stall.

Jackson laughed. "Same to you."

Twenty

Jackson wanted to be out of the house by five-thirty to make certain he was at the airport well ahead of schedule. He hated to be late, even by one minute, for anything. But, picking up Gunnery Sergeant Wyatt Davidson and getting him to the hotel to be with his family wasn't just an ordinary task. He took this as a top priority assignment and would do everything in his power to make sure all went smoothly and according to plan.

He was happy that Jose and George would be taking care of the morning and evening feeding chores for the day. His "To Do" list for Christmas Eve was filled to capacity, but telling Taylor how he felt was at the very top.

Andrew and Beth and Josh and Anna would be arriving at some point in the early afternoon. So, there would be introductions to make along with preparations for an evening Mass and, in the midst of the hubbub, find time for dinner.

He parked his truck, made contact with the limo driver and walked into the terminal. He checked the times on the incoming board and saw that the flight was on time. He turned and walked to the baggage claim area and began his wait for Gunny Davidson.

Thirty minutes later Jackson saw him walking down the ramp toward him.

Jackson reached out to shake Davidson's hand. "Welcome home, Gunny."

He dropped his bag and said, "Brother, a simple handshake just won't do."

They smiled and shared a quick welcome home hug and then the handshake.

"Gunny, Mr. Whitfield's arranged for a limo to take you to the Cedar Towers Hotel and…"

"What! A limo. Hotel? That's not…"

"Gunny, you can't argue with Mr. Whitfield when he's made up his mind about something. Anyway, he said this is his gift to you and your family in thanks for your service to our country."

He shook his head. "I sure wasn't expecting to come home to this."

Jackson grinned. "Well, it gets better. The limo and driver are yours for the day. Of course, you're family's still totally unaware of your homecoming. They're on their way to the Cedar Towers Hotel and a banquet room for what they believe is just a small family get together for the Christmas holiday. That's thanks to your sister-in-law, Marie. She's kept this under wraps from the beginning."

Davidson shook his head and smiled. "This whole thing's just overwhelming. How can I every repay Mr. Whitfield for what he's done."

"Gunny, take my word for it, Mr. Whitfield doesn't expect a thing in return. He told me getting you home to celebrate Christmas with your wife and daughter was reward enough. He said he hopes there'll be plenty of pictures and videos of your welcome home so he can see them later."

"He can count on that. And, I would like to meet him and thank him face to face."

"Gunny, if it fits into your schedule while you're home, Mr. Whitfield wants to have you, Helen and Addie over for dinner one evening between Christmas and New Year's Day."

"Man, it's gonna take time for this to sink in."

"Well, while you're tryin' to hash it over, let's get you on the way to the hotel. I know you wanna be with your family."

Gunnery Sergeant Davidson sat in the backseat of the limo, a large smile on his face and the anticipation of seeing his wife and daughter rising. It felt like it had been a lifetime ago since he'd last held his wife and daughter, kissed them and told them how much he loved them.

Jackson followed the limo to the hotel and there he escorted Gunny Davidson into the lobby. A hotel staff member approached and said he'd take them to the banquet room where his family was waiting.

Jackson said, "Gunny, this is where we part for now."

'You're not gonna come in and see Helen and Addie."

"Gunny, this is your homecoming. I think you should have the time with your family all to yourself. If you have a break in your schedule, we'll get together for a beer while you're home."

Davidson hugged him again and shook his hand. "Count on that, brother. Semper Fi."

"Ooh Rah."

Jackson left the hotel and tried calling Taylor. Again, she did not answer and he decided to call Diane. But, she too failed to pick up, allowing his call to go to voicemail. He left a message saying he needed to get in touch with Taylor.

He checked the schedule for the mayor's gala and found he had plenty of time before the festivities began. He decided he'd make a quick detour and try to catch Father Kurt at St. Martin's before he went to breakfast.

Father Kurt was just leaving the church after the morning Mass when Jackson caught up with him. He gave him a rather hurried run down of his past and that he'd learned only a day ago that he'd been baptized Catholic.

His mother also told him he'd made his first confession and

First Holy Communion, although his memory of those events was very hazy. He said he was aware that it was probably going to be a long road back, but asked if he could try and make a confession.

Father Kurt smiled and they walked back into the church together. With some coaching, Jackson made it through his first confession since early childhood and was assured he could receive communion at the Christmas Mass. Then, Father Kurt told him they could make arrangements sometime after the New Year for him to begin to learn his way back completely.

He left the church and drove to the diner for breakfast. Of course, Barb wanted to know where Taylor was and he tried to pass off a quick explanation, but was sure she didn't believe him.

After breakfast he stopped long enough to pick up another supply of candy canes and then went to meet Sheriff Jennings. It was quickly evident that the sheriff didn't have anything particular for Jackson to do. He simply wanted him to be there to observe one of the many civic functions he'd be performing once he became a deputy.

Jackson made the most of the opportunity, walking around and talking with the children and their parents while he gave them each a candy cane.

Of course, many recognized him from media reports on his meeting Addie Davidson and finding the lost children, Robby and Samantha Swanson. Dozens of parents asked to take his picture with their children, which he readily agreed to and a few parents wanted their photo taken with him as well.

Once again, he tried to call Taylor, but was met with the same results as all his previous calls. He stuffed his phone in his pocket and went about keeping the children on their toes by asking them to name Santa's reindeer. One of the kids turned the table and told him to name all the reindeer.

Jackson surprised not only the children, but also their parents when he rattled off their names. "Dasher, Dancer, Prancer, Vixen,

Comet, Cupid, Donder and Blitzen. And, last but not least, there's Rudolph the Red Nosed Reindeer."

When it was announced that Santa Claus would be arriving soon, calm rapidly switched to bedlam with squeals and screams of delight filling the air.

Jackson was probably as happy or happier than the children to hear the Santa announcement. It very quickly got him off the hook when a child asked him to name the seven dwarfs from Snow White.

***

Taylor left Diane's and returned home and was thankful that no one was there. She wasn't up to talking with her parents, at least not until she was able to pull herself together.

She was still struggling with her emotions over what she'd heard the night before. She tried again and again to think if she saw any indication at all that Jackson had a girlfriend. Yet, try as she might, she couldn't recall even the slightest suggestion that there was another woman in his life.

She went to her room and soon was standing in the shower with rivers of hot water streaming over her. She took her time and washed her hair while she enjoyed the pulsating beads of hot water from the massaging showerhead that beat against her shoulders.

She took extra time in the shower, trying to think of how she would react to meeting Jackson's girlfriend.

Well, as difficult as it might be, I'm gonna do my best to put on my happy face and pretend that everything is just fine. I'll make it through this and start over.

She had just stepped out of the shower and began toweling dry when her phone rang. She was about to ignore it, but saw that it was her father calling.

"Hello, Dad."

"Taylor, your mother and I are…" The phone cut out, but he called back a few seconds later. "Sorry, Taylor. This must be a bad area for reception. Anyway, your mother and I are on the way to the airport to pick up Jackson's…" The phone cut out again, but this time there was no return call.

She shook her head. *My parents… my parents are on the way to the airport to pick up Jackson's girlfriend. Talk about the ultimate slap in the face.*

She fought to keep herself under control. She took a deep breath and clinched her teeth, determined not to allow her emotions to tear down her willpower.

She took her time dressing and went to the kitchen where she drank a cup of coffee. She turned down Juanita's offer to fix a good hearty breakfast for her, but did force herself to eat a slice of fresh baked coffee cake.

She wasn't paying much attention to the time and before she knew it, she heard the front door opening. She felt a brief rush of panic, but quickly composed herself.

She took a deep breath, stood up and began walking to the living room. She opened the door, turned left and saw her parents and a woman close to their age with them.

Her father smiled and said, "Taylor, come over here and meet Jackson's mother."

Taylor stared at the woman for a few seconds before numbly walking toward her. Her mind was reeling, trying to comprehend what she'd just heard.

"Taylor, this is Mary Barton, Jackson's mother," she heard her father say.

She reached out, took Taylor by the hands and looked into her eyes. She smiled, squeezed her hands and said, "So, you're the young woman my son's in love with."

Taylor looked from her to her father, then her mother. Words were on the tip of her tongue, but she was having difficulty trying to speak. Finally, she whispered, "You… You're Jackson's mother?"

She was still holding Taylors hands. "Yes, I am. And I see why Jackson's in love with you. You're certainly everything he said you were."

Suddenly she felt like a fool. "Oh, God, I… I've made a terrible mistake. I thought… I mean… I… I've gotta find Jackson right away." She looked at her father. "Do you know where he is?"

"He's in town with Sheriff Jennings. I believe he was gonna help out with the Mayor's Christmas party for needy children and their families."

She rushed to the hallway, grabbed her coat and was out the door without saying another word.

She started her car while saying, "I can't believe I was this foolish. Why didn't I just answer the phone when he called me last night?" Suddenly, she stopped the car and blurted, "Oh, no. Did I call him in the middle of the night and scream at him or leave him a nasty message? Oh… Oh, I hope that was a dream."

She quickly checked her phone, but found no record that she had called him. She shook her head, wondering if she'd used Diane's phone. But she couldn't remember. Perhaps it was just a bad dream.

"Oh, this whole jumbled mess is a bad dream, Taylor," she muttered. "And you're the guilty party."

All of a sudden, she found herself looking for a place to park, but couldn't remember much of the drive into town. At last she saw a parking space—right next to Jackson's truck.

She looked at the cordoned off area and it was flooded with an ocean of humanity. Young children, older children, teen agers and adults seemed to be moving in dozens of directions and she had no idea where to look for Jackson.

She stopped and muttered, "Come on, Taylor, where would he be?" She scanned the huge venue from left to right and front to back and suddenly saw a crowd of children. Suddenly she laughed. "I know where you are."

She made her way through the mob of people and finally saw him. His back was to her, but she could tell from the smiles on the faces of the children, Jackson Riley was passing out candy canes and was surely running neck and neck with Santa Claus as their favorite.

Certainly, it had to be a miracle, but there was a path through the crowd directly to him. She took off running toward him and as she drew near yelled, "Jackson Riley."

He quickly turned, and just in time to see Taylor leap from the ground. She was now hurtling toward him and as he reached to catch her, she threw her legs around his waist, her arms around his shoulders and crushed her lips to his.

He somehow maintained his balance and turned slowly, as he held tightly to her. It seemed Taylor was determined to see how long she could make the kiss last, and it was very obvious Jackson wasn't trying to escape.

The reaction from the crowd varied according to age, with some "yucks" and "oooohhh, gross" from the youngest to a growing round of applause from the adults.

Taylor finally pulled away and looked into his eyes. "I've been in love with you forever and I'm gonna marry you."

He smiled. "Have we met?"

She began laughing. "Oh, I don't believe you. You did it again. You..."

His lips pressing against hers cut off her reply. The chorus of applause mixed with "yucks" and "gross" began again, but Jackson and Taylor didn't seem to notice.

At some point he put her down and she said, "Jackson, please forgive me. I was..."

"Forgive you? Forgive you for what?"

"I did something very stupid and I..."

He put a finger to her lips. "Shhhhh. Well, I must've missed whatever it was. So, let's forget it. Now, let's get back to the 'I've been in love with you forever and I'm gonna marry you' part. I hope you meant that."

She kissed him quickly and said, "Yes, I meant it. But I was afraid that you might not love me."

"Taylor, I fell in love with you the instant I threw you in the water trough."

She gave him another quick kiss. "If you promise to love me everyday for the rest of my life you can throw me in the water trough once a month."

He shook his head. "I was thinkin' more like once a week."

She laughed again. "Oh, boy, are we ever gonna have a very unique and interesting, relationship. You'll be wanting to throw me in the horse trough once a week and I'll be threatening you with the riding crop. Of course, I wonder how many times you'll compare me to a horses' backside and..."

He grabbed her and kissed her, holding the kiss for almost a minute before stepping back. "Taylor, if I agree that we'll have a unique and interesting relationship, will you stop talkin' long enough for us to go home?" He leaned close and whispered in her ear. "We have a very large audience watching and listening to every word."

She glanced over her shoulder and blushed. "I... I guess I forgot where we were."

They turned and walked hand and hand to the parking lot. He kissed her on the cheek and said, "Let's head back to Whitfield Acres and let everyone know about us and..."

"Jackson, we don't hafta say a word about us being in love. They already know."

"Your parents too?"

"Oh, yes. Mom told me she knew and Dad doesn't hafta to say anything, but he knows."

***

When they arrived at the house, they were surprised to find that Andrew, Beth, Josh and Anna were already there.

Josh and Anna greeted them at the door and very excitedly told them Santa Claus was coming to visit that night. Soon, they had Jackson and Taylor by their hands and doing their best to drag them to the Christmas tree.

"Look! Look!" they shouted. "Santa's already been here and put the tree up."

Jackson laughed. "Oh, you should've seen Santa and his elf tryin' to pick out a tree."

"You saw Santa pick the tree out," Josh gushed.

"I sure did. And, you know what?"

"What?" they said.

"His elf climbed on his shoulders so they could be sure the tree was just right."

"Really?"

"Yes, and the elf pulled Santa's hat down over his eyes and they fell in the snow."

"Wow! They fell in the snow!"

"But they didn't get hurt."

"That's cause snow's soft," Anna said with a nod.

Andrew looked at Taylor. "Okay, little sister, I'd like to hear the whole story about Santa and his elf."

"No. You don't hafta hear it."

Jackson smiled. "Andrew, I'd be happy to tell you all about the Great Christmas Tree Caper later tonight."

"Oh, I can't wait."

"Jackson, don't you dare tell him."

"Don't worry. I wasn't gonna tell Andrew... I'm gonna make sure I tell the whole family. I'm sure you dad and mom would love to hear it again."

Before Taylor could respond, Andrew said, "By the way, I understand you finally found 'Mr. Perfect'."

She smiled and looked at Jackson. "Well, he's not exactly Mr. Perfect but he's certainly Mr. Right."

Jackson laughed and said he had a few things to take care of and left the room.

Andrew looked at Taylor and went on. "Good. I'm very happy for you and I know dad's overjoyed with your choice. He really likes Jackson."

She laughed. "Oh, I found that out very quickly when dad refused to fire him for throwing me in the horse trough."

"I agree with dad, you probably deserved it."

"You think I..." She paused and shook her head. "Yes, I deserved it. In fact, I was probably begging to be thrown in the trough."

"And you got your wish."

"Andrew, what do you think of Jackson?"

"I haven't had that much time to get to know him, but my first impression's always been on the mark. I like him. He seems like a take-charge kinda guy and somebody who isn't afraid to get his hands dirty. And, the way Josh and Anna took to him tells me a lot about his character."

"I'm happy you like him."

The afternoon was busy with everyone seeming as though they were going in opposite directions.

Jackson spent time in the barn preparing the evening feeding and making sure all the water buckets were cleaned and topped off. Then he found some time for grooming Christmas and telling her she'd be meeting his mother later.

Taylor was busy trying to finish wrapping Christmas presents between trips to the closet searching for something appropriate to wear to Mass. All of that while talking on the phone with Diane and telling her how her love life was on the fast track to happiness.

Granddad and grandma entertained Josh and Anna while Andrew and Beth very quietly sneaked packages into the house from their car.

In spite of what appeared to be a ball of confusion in the Whitfield home, everybody managed to meet on time for dinner at four-thirty.

Juanita had prepared a buffet style dinner of baked ham, steamed shrimp, oysters on the half-shell, potato salad, macaroni salad, chicken fingers and macaroni and cheese for Josh and Anna, and an assortment of gingerbread, sugar and chocolate chip cookies for dessert.

After blessing the evening meal Steve announced that anyone who left the table hungry had only themselves to blame.

When dinner was over, it was time to shower and get ready for the eight o'clock Mass at St. Martin's.

Twenty-one

Jackson and Taylor were in her car, with Jackson behind the wheel ready to leave for Mass. The rest of the family would easily find enough room and comfort in Steve's Ford Expedition.

On the drive to St. Martin's Jackson began giving Taylor the condensed version of his childhood. He told her of the issues with his father's drinking and the hardship facing what he called a rein of terror. He went on to tell her of eventual court hearings and the false testimony that took him from his mother. As they were driving on to the parking lot of St. Martin's Church, he was completing the story of his search for and finding of his mother.

The family entered together and Jackson was thrilled to have his mom holding his left arm while Taylor held tightly to his right. They were greeted by the ushers and soon were being taken to their seats.

Much to Jackson's surprise, Bob Swanson walked over to his pew and shook his hand. "I want to thank you again for finding my grandchildren."

"No need to thank me, Mr. Swanson. They're home safe and sound and that's thanks enough. And, I'll tell Christmas you're very grateful for her finding your grandchildren."

"Regardless, I'm deeply grateful for what you did." And by the way, I have honored your request and donated to both causes."

"Thank you, Sir."

Father Kurt was all smiles when he stepped on to the altar, faced the congregation and said, "Merry Christmas."

"Merry Christmas, Father."

The church was filled to capacity and the overflow crowd filled the meeting hall, where the Mass was aired via camera. As always, Father Kurt kept his homily short, but on point telling of the birth of Christ in Bethlehem.

When the Mass ended, they began to slowly make their way out of the church. Father Kurt was waiting to shake the hand of everyone and personally wish them a very Merry Christmas.

While they were moving through the back door, Barb caught Taylor by the arm. "That glow on your face could light up the night. Love agrees with you."

She smiled. "At the moment it's sure making me feel so very happy."

"I told Jackson I expect an invitation to the wedding."

"I'll make sure you're near the top of the list."

When they arrived home, it was close to nine-thirty. Yet, Josh and Anna were positively wild with excitement and rushed to the Christmas tree to see if Santa had already been there. Seeing no gifts, their disappointment was evident, but it was Jackson who quickly turned their mood.

"Santa has to make lots of stops tonight and that means he and his reindeer are gonna be hungry when they get here. So, why don't we go in the kitchen and I'll cut carrots for the reindeer and you fix a plate of cookies for Santa. And, don't forget, I'm sure he'd like some milk."

They carried the plates of cookies and carrots, while Jackson carried the glass of milk into the dining room area. There was a brief discussion as to where the goodies should be placed. Anna thought they should go under the Christmas tree and Josh said they should be left by the fireplace.

Jackson settled the dispute when he suggested they put the plates of carrots and cookies and the glass of milk on the dining room table. The reasons of course were so Santa wouldn't step on the plates and knock over the milk when he came down the chimney. And, he needed the space under the Christmas tree so he could put the presents there.

Now, the next problem arose. They wanted to wait up to see Santa when he arrived.

Taylor took charge at this point. "Josh, Anna, Santa won't stop by until you've gone to bed. And, if you stay up too late, he might not stop here at all."

"Mommy, I'm tired and I wanna go to bed," Anna said.

Josh chimed in. "Me too, mommy."

While Beth was taking them upstairs and getting them ready for bed, Jackson's mother turned to Steve and Rose. "I can't thank you enough for your kind hospitality."

"No need to thank us," Rose said. "It's a pleasure having you here."

"That's right," Steve added.

"I'm astounded by everything that's happened over the past several days. So much happiness has been brought into my life and I know there's more to come. My son found me, I've met the young lady he loves and her family and I feel the warmth and love in this house. And, it's the warmth and love that makes this house a home."

Steve raised his glass of scotch. "Here's to the future and the happiness yet to come."

Beth returned just in time for the toast and when the glasses were lowered, she smiled and asked Jackson to tell the story of the Great Christmas Tree Caper.

Over a very weak protest from Taylor, Jackson once again told the tale of the search for the Whitfield family Christmas tree.

Of course, there was a boisterous round of laughter as the story went on.

When Jackson finished the story, Steve said, "That's only half the tale. Everybody should've been here for the placing and decorating of the tree."

"Oh, I can't wait to hear this," Andrew said.

"Well, to begin with, it was so entertaining I went out and popped some popcorn and got a cold beer."

"It was that entertaining," Rose said. "Believe me."

Now, Steve was the storyteller, pouring out a very detailed description of the event. He had a deadpan way of telling the tale that added even more humor and laughter. When the tale ended he was given a round of applause.

"Jackson, you look very happy, happier than I've seen since you first arrived here," Rose said.

He smiled. "When I arrived in Cedar Falls I felt there was something missing, but I wasn't sure what I was looking to find." He paused for a few seconds while he looked around the room at everyone. "I know this might sound like a strange request, especially at this time of night. But, I want everyone to walk to the barn with me because there's a horse there that's a very intricate part of this."

They knew Juanita was working late in the kitchen putting together the final pieces for tomorrow's dinner. So, the children wouldn't be alone in the house.

Soon, everyone had their coats, hats and gloves and were following Jackson to the barn. He walked hand in hand with Taylor and pulled her closer to him as they neared the barn.

He opened the door, stepped inside and turned on the lights. Almost immediately the barn came to life, horses stirring, "talking" and some tapping grain buckets with their nose. The dogs and cats peeked out from the tack room and Rooster and Rita ran to greet everybody. The cats, of course, expected that if everyone wanted to see them, they'd walk to their domain.

It took a minute or two to make their way to the far end of the barn, but at last they were standing by Christmas's stall. She was already waiting, head out over the gate and looking at Jackson.

"Mom, this is Christmas," he said, taking his mother's hand and leading her to the stall gate.

"Oh, my what a beautiful horse. She's positively gorgeous."

Christmas nodded her head up and down three times, which brought a chuckle from all.

Jackson kissed her on the nose and gave her a spiced apple treat. "The day I drove into Cedar Falls the last thing I expected was that I'd have a horse within fifteen minutes. But, as Mr. Whitfield said it was fate or the wish of the Almighty that I happened to stop by the horse auction.

"I certainly didn't realize at the time what that day was going to mean in the near future. But it was a day that changed my life. I met Mr. and Mrs. Whitfield and Juanita and before I knew it I had a place to stay and job to keep me busy."

Christmas rested her chin on his shoulder and he gently ran his hand along her face. "Now, I spent lots of time at night down here in the barn, grooming this beautiful girl and talking to her. And, I told her I was happy, but something was missing.

"Then I met Taylor." He looked at her and smiled. "We had a brief exchange of pleasantries before I picked her up and tossed her in the horse trough. As I told her today that's when I fell in love with her. And, still, there was something missing and I was at a loss as to what it was I was trying to find.

"I'd been wanting to find my mother and not too long after I arrived here I began an all-out effort to locate her. And, as all of you know I found her only a few days ago."

He shook his head smiled. "Tonight, at Mass I felt so very different. I wasn't sure why until we came back to the house. I lost something a long time ago and I'd been searching for it ever since. But tonight, I knew I'd found what was missing."

He paused and looked at Christmas. "This very beautiful, very intelligent horse was the key to my future. If not for her we wouldn't be here tonight. Finding her brought me to Whitfield Acres where I found Taylor and met each of you. And finally I was able to locate my Mom. Maybe I should've called her Christmas Miracle. Christmas came into my life and took me to find what I wanted most... a family. You... all of you," he said, looking from one to another, "you're my family."

Mary and Rose, who were standing next to each other, were soon sharing an embrace and shedding a few tears. Taylor hugged and kissed Jackson, Beth held Andrew tightly and Steve, well he just stood by, taking it all in and smiling. After all, he'd set the stage for much of the future when he brought Jackson and Christmas back to Whitfield Acres.

Jackson hugged and kissed his mother, telling her again how happy he was to have found her. Next it was hugs for Rose and Beth and a handshake with Andrew and Steve.

After another round of hugs, kisses, a few more tears and handshakes, only Taylor and Jackson remained at the barn.

Taylor was looking at Jackson when she felt a gentle nudge on her back, pushing her into Jackson's arms.

She glanced over her shoulder and said, "Thank you very much, Christmas. This time I'll take the hint."

Jackson pulled her closer while looking beyond her shoulder at Christmas and saying, "Good girl." Then he kissed Taylor.

When he stepped back, he smiled and told Taylor to look over her shoulder. Christmas was shaking her head up and down and had a gleam in her eyes that said she knew from the very beginning that Jackson and Taylor belonged together.

Tonight, Christmas would get a special reward after a final apple treat. First Jackson and then Taylor kissed her on the nose and said goodnight.

Jackson turned out the lights and they walked outside into the cold night air. He put his arm around Taylor as they slowly walked toward the house. There was a breeze whispering through the pines and causing their limbs to gently sway.

They stopped and looked up into the night sky as the clouds parted, revealing one very bright shining star.

"Long, long ago a brilliantly glowing star in Bethlehem gave the world a new beginning," Jackson said, pulling Taylor closer and hugging her tightly. "I believe we can say that this one beautiful star that peeked out from behind the clouds did it only for us."

Taylor looked into his eyes. "Yes, it did. It's telling us this is our beginning."

Made in the USA
Middletown, DE
27 October 2023

41429537R00130